All Books by Harper Lin

Crêpe Murder

A Patisserie Mystery
Book #4

by Harper Lin

ISBN-13: 978-0993949524

ISBN-10: 0993949525

Contents

Recipes

Chapter 1

Clémence Damour and her head baker, Sebastien Soulier, had just made another batch of their latest invention. It was a croissant, but not just any average buttery French croissant. This one had an American influence.

"Are you sure you want to make an *apple pie* croissant?" Sebastien peered at the limp, flaky pastries on the tray and wrinkled his nose. "These are not quite right, either. I don't even have to try them."

This was their third batch of the day. The first batch had been too sweet and overpowering. Clémence thought the second batch had promise until she took a bite and realized it was too crunchy. And now the third batch simply looked weird.

"They're more like apple turnovers," Sebastien continued. "It's going to be a challenge to get the right balance of apples and cinnamon in a light-as-air croissant."

Clémence took a bite. She liked the taste of the croissant, to her surprise. She had always enjoyed American-style pastries and desserts, since she was half American herself, but because their customers were mostly French, their products couldn't be too greasy, dense, or sweet.

"You might as well try one," Clémence said.

"Fine." Reluctantly, Sebastien chewed. "The apples are a little too mushy. Are you sure you want to stick with Granny Smith apples? I'm thinking we can branch out with something more unique, like Pink Lady apples."

"My grandmother in Boston always uses Granny Smith apples. In her apple pies, that is."

"But we're not making an American pastry here. We're trying to come up with something to appeal to the French. Pink Lady apples are a good balance of sweet and tart. We might be able to cut down on some of the sugar in the recipe, too."

Clémence took another bite, just to be sure. The apples were mushier than she would've liked. They had used too much cinnamon this time, too. It was close, but not quite right. Trying a different apple could help tweak the taste a bit.

"I'm open to trying different apples," she said. "Why don't I go to the open-air market tomorrow morning and pick up a few different tart apples? We'll continue this experiment tomorrow."

Sebastien smiled in relief. "*Merci*. I'm glad you're in agreement, for once."

Clémence and Sebastien had a great working relationship, but sometimes they differed in taste. While they ultimately agreed on what made the cut and what didn't, sometimes they had to make compromises in getting to the end product.

"We can also try cutting the apples into thinner slices," Clémence said. "Maybe it'll help cut down on the density."

"Yes, I was just going to suggest that, too."

Sebastien lifted the tray from the table to chuck the croissants in the garbage, but Clémence stopped him.

"Come on," said Clémence. "They're not that bad. They're still good enough for the average person to consume."

"Right." Sebastien chuckled. "The average person."

As bakers, they both had perfectionist tendencies in the kitchen. Anybody else would've thought that the croissants were delicious. Sebastien and Clémence held themselves to a much higher standard. Damour was, after all, one of the best patisseries in Paris.

This was Sebastien's first year working as head baker. He had ambitions to ultimately be one of the *Meilleurs Ouvriers de France*, the best craftsmen in France. It was a prestigious award, and he wanted to win in the pastry chef category. While he was already talented, he wanted to perfect his craft before he entered. This meant he had to work extra hard to be innovative, while adhering to the classic expectations of French consumers. It was a fine balance that Clémence would overstep had she worked alone. This was why she was so grateful to have Sebastien and the team while her parents, the founders of Damour, were in Asia for the next few months.

Clémence looked at her watch. "It's almost four. I'm off."

"Where are you going so early in the work day?"

"I want to check out this painting class," said Clémence. "My friend Ben recommended it. The teacher said I could drop by and see what they're working on."

"I thought you already have a degree in painting," said Sebastien. "Why are you taking more classes?"

"That was for classical painting and art history. Sure, I learned the techniques, but I always feel confined when I paint in some old master's style. It's beautiful, but I've decided that it's not the kind of style I want to pursue. The teacher is from Brazil, and I hear she's more open minded and experimental. Maybe she'll help me loosen up and find my own style."

"Sounds good. You know, I haven't seen any of your artwork. Is it online anywhere?"

"No," said Clémence. "I haven't done anything I'm that proud of yet, so I won't show them until I start producing some good pieces."

"That's funny," said Sebastien. "You're always experimenting and open to trying new things in the kitchen, but you make it sound like you're the opposite when you're in front of the easel."

"Ironic, isn't it? It's some sort of blockage. Maybe it's just years of art teachers telling me I'm doing things all wrong."

"Same here with culinary school. One of my teachers was terrifying."

"Then how did you get to be so open?"

"Your parents really helped," said Sebastien. "Observing how your mom and dad worked in the kitchen. I don't know if you remember, but I was quite conventional in the kitchen when I first started. Your parents really encouraged me to experiment."

Clémence beamed. "That's good to hear. They've always been supportive. I think it helps that my mom had an American upbringing, where there's an emphasis on encouragement rather than pointing out faults."

"How are they by the way? Are they still in Japan?"

"I think they're back in Hong Kong. They're overseeing the recipes for the *salon de thé*. You should see the menu. Dad e-mailed it to me last night. It's Chinese-French fusion food, and there's even French-inspired dim sum. I can't imagine how it tastes."

"That sounds amazing. It'd be so neat to go to a Damour in a different country. I wonder if it'll be like a parallel universe, with different versions of ourselves."

Clémence laughed. "Probably. I can imagine a Chinese version of you in the Hong Kong kitchen, intensely focused on making a jasmine tea macaron or something."

She put the remaining six apple pie croissants in a plastic container.

"Feeding the homeless?" Sebastien asked.

"Something like that," Clémence replied.

In fact, she was planning on giving them to Arthur Dubois, her official boyfriend of two weeks. He was a neighbor. His family lived on the third floor of her building. A PhD student, Arthur lived in one of the *chambres de bonne*, a single room on the top floor, where the servants used to live back in the old days.

Arthur had a big family. There were seven kids in the Dubois household in total. Arthur and his brother Theo both lived in *chambres de bonne*, which were comparable to dorm rooms, while the other siblings lived in the main apartment. His parents still didn't know that Clémence was dating Arthur. Clémence's parents didn't know, either. The young couple wanted their relationship to remain under wraps for the time being, since they were still getting to know each other and didn't want to experience pressure or scrutiny from their elders. She liked the way things were going in the relationship, and didn't want to rush anything. For now, they were simply enjoying each other's company.

She said good-bye to Sebastien and the rest of the staff in the kitchen, and then passed through the *salon de thé* on her way out. Since it was midafternoon, the customers were mostly drinking coffee or tea and eating desserts. She smiled as she passed them, while taking a peek at what they were eating.

A cute girl with her brown hair cut in a pixie style caught her eye. She had big brown eyes, dimples, and looked to be in her mid-twenties. Short hair was hard to pull off, but it suited the girl's feminine features.

There was also something familiar about her. Had Clémence met or seen her somewhere before? Maybe she was a celebrity. It wasn't unusual to see celebrities eating at Damour. Just last week, Marion Cotillard and Guillaume Canet were spotted eating lunch there. Her friend Celine, one of the hostesses, had almost fainted. She was a huge fan of Guillaume Canet and had nearly been hysterical when she ran back into the kitchen to tell Clémence and Berenice who was in the salon.

As Clémence passed by the pixie-haired brunette, she glanced at what she was eating: a dark chocolate crêpe with *chantilly*–whipped cream–and strawberries on the side. She had good taste, as it was also the crêpe of Clémence's choice.

She had been so distracted by the girl and her crêpe that she didn't notice the man she was dining with until it was too late. He was also eating a dark chocolate crêpe. She looked up, inadvertently making eye contact with him.

Carlos. She knew him. Tall, dark haired, square jawed, a muscular build. He was as handsome as a prince, and certainly charming, especially when he spoke with such a sexy Spanish accent. She'd thought she would never see him again. What was he doing in Paris?

Chapter 2

Clémence and Carlos both averted eye contact immediately. He became preoccupied with cutting a piece of his crêpe, and Clémence couldn't get away fast enough.

She had met Carlos almost two years ago, a month after she started her travels around the world. In a fancy hotel bar in Berlin, Carlos came over and introduced himself, saying that he was visiting from Madrid. Clémence and her two American friends, Jessica and Emily, whom she'd been traveling with at the time, all thought Carlos was cute. He was also a bit mysterious, as he didn't reveal details about himself freely.

Apparently he was on vacation, traveling around Europe alone. After a fun evening with the girls, he decided to come along with them to Hungary at the last minute. Carlos dressed in designer clothes and wore a Rolex, so she assumed he was well off. When Emily pressed him for more details about himself, he'd smoothly insinuated that he was a person of importance, but that he was traveling incognito so bodyguards weren't necessary.

When they were back in their hotel room, the girls speculated whether he was Spanish royalty or a rich heir with a lot of time to waste. While the three girls were all well off, they had started out the trip with the intention of staying in hostels to meet other international travelers and to really get into the backpacking experience. But now that they had met Carlos, they were more than happy to change their plans to stay at the five-star hotels that he recommended, figuring that spending time with Spanish royalty would be a more memorable experience.

Clémence found him intriguing as well. Carlos certainly carried himself in a royal manner. He was a gentleman, knew his wines and table etiquette, and everyone in the hotels treated him with the utmost respect. He was also a welcome distraction since she was fresh from a breakup with her ex, Mathieu. Carlos was flirtatious with all of them, but Clémence thought he was interested in her because he'd asked her the most questions.

She told him that she was an artist, but that she was traveling around the world to gain some real-life experience and to find inspiration. She left out the part about being the heiress of Damour, a multi-million dollar company. Had she told him her real last name, and not her mother's maiden name, Fontaine, he would've found pictures of her online, since she used to be part of the Paris socialite scene with Mathieu.

Part of the reason Clémence was traveling was to escape from that life she shared with her ex. Plus she figured if Carlos was going to be secretive, she didn't want to lay all her cards out on the table, either.

Carlos and the girls all had innocent fun together, visiting tourist attractions and hitting the bars and restaurants, while meeting other travelers along the way. He taught them some Spanish, and they teased him for his accent while gushing about how sexy it was behind his back.

Clémence was starting to fall for Carlos by the end of their second week traveling together. In Budapest, he kissed her in a nightclub after they escaped out to the terrace alone while they were both drunk and more uninhibited. Carlos asked her more questions about herself, and Clémence revealed that she'd grown up in Romainville, a suburb of Paris. When she pressed him for more details about who he was, he remained vague, saying he was a real nobody, nobody she'd care to know.

Clémence laughed, thinking it was a funny joke at the time because he'd just paid a grand for their private table in the V.I.P. section of the club, which included two bottles of outrageously expensive champagne.

The next morning, something strange happened. Carlos vanished. He simply checked out. That was what the concierge at the hotel told them. He was gone, just like that. Clémence didn't even get his e-mail address, last name, or anything.

It turned out that he had also kissed Emily on the same night. When the two girls compared notes, they all thought it was odd. What did Carlos want with them, really? He had not tried to sleep with them; he seemed more interested in chatting than anything else.

It took a couple of weeks for Clémence to get over the disappointment and to forget about him. At least she had not gone to bed with the guy, which would've made her feel much worse.

Jessica and Emily were still convinced he was a Spanish royal out for some anonymous fun, and they tried to find proof on the Internet. They examined pictures of the royal family and searched for extended family members in the backgrounds of weddings and royal events. There were a couple of princes who did look like Carlos, but they couldn't find Carlos himself.

Clémence wasn't so convinced. While it wasn't impossible, she thought he was probably a normal guy. A normal guy with a lot of money to throw around.

Maybe he'd fallen for both her and Emily, and didn't want to come between the two friends, so he left. That was a generous explanation.

In any case, Clémence vowed after that to be more cautious with guys. At the time, it had seemed fun and carefree to be out and about with a rich, handsome stranger, but the experience taught her to find out more about guys before she fell for them.

When Clémence reached the front door of Damour, she took Celine aside to ask her about Carlos.

"There's a guy sitting in table five," said Clémence. "I sort of know him, but not really. Anyway, long story short, I want to find out more about him. What do you know about this guy?"

"I don't know much," said Celine. "This is the first time I've seen him here too, although Sophie Seydoux has been here plenty of times."

"Sophie Seydoux? I know that name, I think."

"She's a socialite. I thought you knew who she was. Her family owns the *Chateau du Chocolat* stores."

"A chocolate heiress?" Clémence was amused. "She does look familiar."

"She's in the tabloids all the time. I love her new haircut."

"Yes, she's pretty. I thought she was an actress or something."

"I suppose she's going out with this guy. He's gorgeous too. He spoke with a Spanish accent, but I didn't get his name, since they didn't make a reservation." Celine paused and cocked her head at her. "You're not investigating a murder case or something, are you?"

"God no," said Clémence. "We've gone a few weeks without a murder now, and I'm still recovering. I just know this guy, sort of, and I want to find out who he is. I'll tell you the full story later because I have to run, but can you try to find out his last name at least?"

"Sure. Maybe he'll pay by credit card and we'll find out without much hassle."

"Great," said Clémence. "Thanks a million. *À plus tard.*"

Chapter 3

Clémence art class was in the 9th arrondissement near Rue des Martyr. When she found the address, she looked through the window and saw sewing machines on worktables and half-finished dresses on mannequins. It was a sewing workshop, not a painting class. She tapped on the window to get the attention of the sole person inside.

A woman with dyed orange hair, wearing a red and white striped Rockabilly-style dress, opened the door with a smile.

"*Bonjour.* Can I help you?"

"*Oui, bonjour.* I'm looking for Madame Amaro's painting class. Am I at the right address?"

"You'll have to go through the gate, but you need a code. I'll come out and help you."

The gate was next to the sewing classroom, and the woman punched in the code. "Go on in."

"*Merci.*"

Clémence passed through the small garden of the front entrance. Wild flowers grew, and so did the weeds. It was a bit untamed, imperfect, but maybe it was symbolic of what she wanted to accomplish there.

The receptionist at the front desk, a bespectacled woman in her late fifties who was more sensibly dressed, was on the phone when Clémence came in. When she hung up, she looked up at Clémence.

"Welcome to the Spinoza Atelier," she said. "Are you here for a class?"

"Catia Amaro told me that it was okay to drop in and check out her art class. Is it in this building?"

"Certainly. It's on the second floor. Room Five. This is your first time here?"

"*Oui.*"

"We have all sorts of classes here for people of all ages. Pottery, dance, sculpting, jewelry making—you name it." The woman gave her a pamphlet. "Here are all the classes listed and our spring and summer schedule, including the painting class for Madame Amaro. If you have any questions, feel free to ask."

"Thanks so much."

Clémence passed by a sculpting class before she came to the staircase. The class was for children around twelve, and they seemed to be making a mess of the clay, but most of them were concentrating very hard on their work. On the second floor, she passed by a hip-hop dance class and a printmaking class. When she found Room Five, she poked her head in through the crack of the door.

A woman in her forties, with long, curly black hair and silver bangles piled on both wrists, was walking from easel to easel, critiquing the painters. Although she'd only spoken to Catia Amaro on the phone, Clémence could tell it was her by the commanding way she moved and gestured the canvases, and by how the students listened to her attentively.

Catia had plenty of meat on her bones. She was dressed in a leopard-print maxi dress and wore more necklaces than she had on bangles. Clémence tried to imagine wearing that much jewelry herself. She'd probably fall over by the sheer weight.

"Clémence, is that you?" Catia called out to her. "Come on in. Don't be shy."

Clémence stepped in. "*Bonjour à tous.* Hi everyone. *Je suis Clémence.*"

The six students smiled and greeted her back. They were of all different ages. The closest person to her age was a girl who looked to be in her early twenties.

"Here to critique our work?" joked a man in his sixties wearing suspenders over his blue plaid shirt.

"More like to admire your work," said Clémence said. "That's beautiful."

She referred to the man's dreamy shades of blue on a square canvas, and the gray strokes that formed what looked like a boat.

"Clémence might be joining our class," said Catia. "So be on your best behavior. Butter her up a bit."

The class laughed.

"We have students of all levels," Catia continued. "Albert here has been painting for years."

"Longer than you've lived," the senior joked again.

"His wife Rita just started," said Catia.

"You can probably tell, right?" Rita gave an apologetic look. Her painting was full of squares in primary colors.

"No," Clémence protested. "That looks very Mondrian."

Rita beamed. "Why, thank you, dear."

"And Amelie started painting a year ago," Catia said, walking towards the young woman. "She's studying art restoration."

"Amazing work," said Clémence.

Amelie's painting was of a small cabin in a forest during the night. The moon was out, and the cabin's light was on. It was one of the more conventional paintings, but Clémence recognized the skill.

"You've only been painting for a year?" Clémence asked. "Are you sure?"

"Yes, I'm just doing this for fun, really. I'd like to work for Le Louvre in their restoration department someday."

"Cool."

The work of the other three students were quite interesting, as well. One abstract painting in shades of red depicted anger and confusion. Another was an experimental still life of a chair in double vision. The third was of a mouth and a train track going down into the throat.

"An exploration of the body's journey," explained a rail-thin man with an Irish accent.

Clémence nodded and smiled. "Can't wait to see it completed."

"I wanted to keep the class small," Catia said to Clémence. "So I can work with each artist individually as the class time permits. The class is two times a week, Tuesdays and Thursdays. Bring your own canvas, but we have easels, paints, and brushes at your disposal, unless you want to bring your own. My philosophy is that everyone can paint. Art is an exploration of the soul, and I want to bring out each person's talents, at whatever level they're at. If I see that they need to develop certain techniques, I give them certain exercises."

"Sounds good," said Clémence. "I'd love to join you for the next class."

"Great! Have you decided what subject matter you'd like to tackle first?"

Clémence grinned. She'd been thinking about this for a while, but she hadn't had time with all the murder investigations. Ben had been bugging her about painting more, and Clémence figured that classes would help her stick to a schedule. It would also help to get perspective from a teacher and inspiration from fellow students. Catia's class seemed like the perfect place to start.

"I was thinking about doing a series of paintings of desserts," Clémence said. "I want to call it The Sweet Life."

Clémence met Arthur at Île de la Cité, where they had a rendezvous to picnic. It was June, and the day had been sunny so far. She crossed her fingers that the sun would stay out. There had been a lot of rainy days in the past few weeks, so as soon as the clouds parted, the entire city came out to make the most of it.

Île de la Cité was a sizeable island on the Seine in central Paris, where the Notre Dame Cathedral was also located. The island was easily accessible by bridges connecting to both the left bank and the right bank. Arthur and Clémence had agreed to meet at the tip of the island, a popular picnic spot with shady trees and a magnificent view of the city and the Seine river.

Arthur had come from the library, having spent the day at the university library working on his PhD in macroeconomics. He already had a blanket spread out and was lying down with his hands supporting the back of his head.

With his sunglasses on and a five o'clock shadow, Arthur looked more ruggedly handsome than usual. Clémence sat down and leaned over him to give him a kiss, which woke him up.

"That tired?" Clémence laughed.

"Clémence. Thank god it's you. For a moment I thought it was some other gorgeous girl kissing me."

She smacked him playfully on the chest. "What you got there? Champagne and strawberries?"

"That and more." Arthur sat up, pushing his sunglasses up to his chestnut brown hair. His warm brown eyes shone with joy as he reached into the grocery bag from *La Grande Épicerie*, a gourmet supermarket that Clémence adored. He pulled out a fresh baguette, black caviar, Camembert cheese, cream cheese, sliced sausages, and the strawberries and champagne.

"Oh, we did some experimenting at work today." She gave him the apple pie croissants. "Eat them later, or give them to your family."

"Where would I say I got them from?"

"Just say a friend made them. It's the truth. I'm starved. Where's the cutlery? I want to start eating right away."

Arthur's face fell. "Oh the cutlery. I totally forgot. And the cups too. We'll have to take swigs out of the bottle."

"You did? Oh. Well I suppose we can just use my fingers, although my hands are kind of dirty..."

"Totally kidding." Arthur grinned. "I brought cutlery from home." He took out some fancy silverware from another bag, along with plastic cups shaped like wine glasses. "I found them in our cupboard. I didn't even know they made plastic cups like these."

"That's because you don't do your own shopping," Clémence teased. "I'm impressed. And if I ever see you doing your own laundry, I'll have a heart attack."

"Hey, I can be competent when I want to be. But I'm a busy man. I'll only work when there's a reward."

Clémence raised an eyebrow at him. "And I'm the reward?"

"The reward is to see you happy." He pulled her in closer on the blanket and kissed her on the cheek.

It was hard to believe that she and Arthur had used to hate each other. She once thought that he was a complete snob, and he used to find her annoying, but since they started running into each other more after Clémence moved in to house-sit, they were always somehow thrown together to solve murder cases. Gradually, they grew on each other.

They had plenty of sexual chemistry, but Clémence was still getting to know him. She wasn't sure if they were completely compatible, since Arthur was the logical, book-smart type, and Clémence was creative and spontaneous.

"Tell me something I don't know about you," said Clémence. "I want to learn one new fact about you every day."

Arthur thought about it. "I used to play the piano."

"Really? No way!"

"Yup. My mother forced me. From age four to fifteen. I had to go to piano lessons twice a week and practice all the time, even though I drove my siblings crazy."

"So you must be good then."

"I was, and I was seriously considering doing it as a profession before I realized how much I hated it."

"Hated it? But why?"

"Because I didn't choose it. Practice was torture, and after a while, I just stopped hearing the music."

"So you lost your passion."

"Completely. But now I don't hate it as much since I'm not under so much pressure anymore. Sometimes I'll play a song for the family here and there."

Clémence shook her head. "I can't believe you're a pianist. That's so surprising. I guess I never thought of you as the musical type."

"Well, piano, or music in general, is all about mathematics. And I have a musical ear, so I was a quick learner."

"I'd love to hear you play one day. In a proper tux and everything."

"I'll play *Clair de Lune*, and you'll swoon." Arthur grinned.

"Like all the other girls you've serenaded?" Clémence teased.

"Hardly. Except once, when I was fifteen. In high school, I brought this girl I was trying to impress home one day and played the song I was learning at the time."

"Was she impressed?"

"Of course. I got a kiss out of that."

"Maybe if I ever get to come over to your house, you can play for me. You know, if our families ever find out we're dating, and we're still together by then."

Clémence regretted what came out of her mouth as soon as she said it.

Arthur frowned. "Of course we'll be together. Actually, I wouldn't mind telling my mother, if that's what you want."

"No. I mean, it's fine. I like the way it is now. It's only been two weeks. Why rush things?"

He relaxed a bit and hugged her closer. "Okay then. It's going well, and I don't want anything to ruin this, either. So how did your day go? You went to the art class?"

"Yes. I signed up for the semester. I'm looking forward to painting again. I've been so busy with work, and all the recent drama has been so stressful. Rose is living in Germany now, and I'm just getting back into the swing of things."

"I'm glad you're doing something you like again. It would be a nice change if weird things stopped happening in Paris."

Clémence was reminded of Carlos earlier that morning. "Do you know that socialite Sophie Seydoux?"

"As a matter of fact, I do. She's a couple of years younger than me, but Theo knows her. They went to the same school together, and they're pretty good friends. I've also met Sophie and her sister at various social gatherings, like Theo's birthday parties. Why do you ask?"

"I just saw her at Damour earlier, dining with this guy Carlos." She told Arthur the whole story about how she knew Carlos. "I can't believe I traveled with him for almost two weeks without finding out more about him. I don't even know his last name."

"That's odd. Maybe he's married or had a girl-friend or something. Hey, you didn't do anything crazy on your travels, did you?"

Arthur tried to sound casual, but Clémence could tell he really wanted to know.

"No," Clémence said honestly. "Not at all. You know my relationship history. And I sure know yours."

Clémence and Arthur had spent one of their long evenings together talking, and the conver-sation had turned to past lovers. While Clémence had three boyfriends before him, Arthur only had one relationship, but a series of flings, the number of which did not make Clémence happy. However, it wasn't as if Arthur's old playboy ways came as a shock. She was well aware of his past, which had made her hesitant about being with him to begin with. Now, he was devoted to her and only wanted to be with her, and that was what she chose to focus on.

"Forget about this Carlos guy," said Arthur.

"I'm just curious who he is. He insinuated that he was royalty or something, so my friends and I thought he was so mysterious."

"He's probably just some spoiled rich kid who likes to throw money around and feel important."

Clémence laughed and shoved a piece of baguette with cream cheese and caviar in his mouth. "Takes one to know one, right?"

Arthur began tickling her, and she squealed, catching looks from other picnickers nearby.

"Stop." She giggled and tried to swat him away.

"Carlos is probably not even this guy's real name," he continued. "He's dating Sophie now. Big deal. He's probably in the same scene."

"It was just really awkward to see him. I wonder if he's living in Paris and if I'll have to run into him more often. Maybe I'll finally find out why he just disappeared on us."

"So you love a good mystery when it comes to men too, huh? I should start being more mysterious. Maybe you'll like me more."

"I already like you plenty. And no, I've so over mystery. I'll take an honest, open guy any day." She looked deep into his eyes. "Seriously."

He kissed her. They slowly leaned back on the trunk of the tree, still kissing, as the sun began to set.

Chapter 4

"I've got info," Celine told to Clémence as soon as Clémence came in to work.

"Really? What's the scoop?"

"Well, first of all, we didn't get his name because he paid in cash—a hundred-euro bill, no less."

"Oh, too bad."

"But when Sophie went to the restroom, he asked about you."

"Me? He asked you about me?"

"No, he asked Christine." Celine referred to one of the waitresses. "He asked her who was the girl with the dark bob and the striking blue eyes. Christine, thinking that he was interested in you, bragged a little and told him that you were the owner of the Damour chain."

Clémence's face fell. "She did that?"

"Was she not supposed to do that?"

Clémence shrugged. "I guess in a way it's common knowledge who I am, but now he knows more about me than I know about him."

"Christine asked him who he was, but he looked around before saying his name was Carlos. He seemed a bit nervous when Sophie came back from the restroom. Christine thought it might've been because he didn't want his date to know that he was inquiring about some other girl. What is going on? Do you guys have history?"

"Sort of." Clémence told her the story about Carlos.

"Another mystery to solve," Celine joked. "That's weird that he left. Some men are just callous. But I have to admit, he is really cute. No wonder Sophie's going out with him, especially if he's a secret prince or something."

"I don't know about that," said Clémence. "I'll just ask Arthur's brother Theo to ask Sophie who he is. Theo went to school with her. I guess Carlos did remember me. It was such an awkward encounter. There's something odd about this whole thing."

"Well, you'll get to the bottom of this soon. You always do."

Clémence worked in the kitchen for the whole morning, helping Sebastien and Berenice with their new macaron flavors. At noon, she took a shopping cart to head to Marché de l'Alma, an open-air market that lasted only a few hours. She could've asked one of her employees or interns to pick up the apples, but she loved going to the market. Everything was fresh and colorful, and she wouldn't mind eating some paella from one of the stalls there for lunch.

All the trees on Avenue de Président Wilson were lush and green, after the flowers had fallen off. There were still a few petals in the gutters. Tourists with maps were everywhere. Clémence chuckled. Some of them were probably looking for Place du Trocadéro to see the Eiffel Tower, which was only around the corner. Sure enough, a German couple stopped her to ask for directions.

The market was bustling, as usual, with locals and tourists alike. Fruit vendors were calling out prices at the entrance. Clémence stopped to admire the roses and sunflowers at a flower stall, then proceeded past the seafood to stop at her favorite fruit seller to buy apples.

"*Bonjour*, Sarah," she said to the seller, who was a woman in her fifties. "I'm looking for some apples for baking."

Sarah recommended a few from her selection. The Pink Lady apples ended up costing a fortune. Clémence also bought Honeycrisp and Mutsu apples. All the apples took up half the shopping cart and weighed a ton. She dragged the cart to the paella stand, where she bought a container to take away. After she poked around the rest of the stalls, which sold everything from old postcards to homemade honey, yogurts, and cheeses, her cart was full of fresh fruit, vegetables, and homemade goods.

At Place d'Iena, she sat on a bench to eat her paella as people lined up for the Musee de Guimet behind her.

After she finished her meal and when she was about to stand to throw away her empty container, a man walked up to her.

"Clémence?"

She was in shock as she looked into the dark eyes of Carlos.

"Carlos? What are you doing here?"

"I thought it was you." He greeted her, kissing her on the cheeks. "May I?" He gestured the empty spot on the bench next to her.

Clémence didn't know where to begin. She had so many questions. Luckily Carlos started talking without any prompting.

"I saw you yesterday at the restaurant, and I didn't know if it was you, so I asked the waitress. They said you owned the Damour chain. Why didn't you tell me you owned the patisserie that makes my favorite macarons?"

"Well, my parents really own the place. I saw you yesterday, too, and I didn't know whether I should've said hello, since you were with a date and we hadn't been in touch for so long. Plus, I didn't know what had happened to you when you left a couple of years ago."

"About that—I'm glad I ran into you because I want to apologize. I really had a lot of fun with you girls and I would've loved to stay, but there was a family emergency and I had to go. My mother had fallen ill. She's okay now, but she had a brain tumor that had to be removed, so I flew back to Spain the next morning as soon as she called me. I left a message with the concierge to tell you that I left, but it sounds like they didn't give it to you. I was going to send you a text message, but someone stole my phone when I got to the airport, so I didn't even have contacts for any of you girls. I'm so sorry."

"Oh." Clémence took a moment to take it all in. "I'm sorry about your mother. We were wondering what had happened. I take it everything's okay with your mother now?"

"Yes, she's fine. Made a full recovery."

"That night, you kissed Emily, right? And then me. On the same night."

She didn't mean to sound accusatory, so she pressed a smile. She just wanted to find out what he had been thinking.

"I was a little drunk that night," said Carlos. "You are all beautiful girls, and I went a little overboard. I'm sorry. But I've matured since then. Now I'm in love."

"With the girl you were with yesterday? Sophie?"

"Yes." He beamed. "Do you know her?"

"Not directly. But I know of her. Does that mean you're staying in Paris now?"

"Yes. I'm living with her. She has really changed me. Oh, by the way, Carlos is my middle name. I go by Juan. Juan Carlos Camondo."

"Oh. Okay. I should start calling you Juan then?"

"Yes, because Juan is my real first name. I wanted to change it to Carlos, but I realized that it didn't suit me."

"Okay, Juan."

"What about you? Are you seeing anyone?"

"I am." She nodded. "His name is Arthur."

"Maybe we can all go to dinner sometimes," said Juan.

"Really?"

"Sure. I'm new in the city, and I'm in need of friends. Can I take your number? I'll ask Sophie to see what she says."

"Okay." Clémence also took his number. She seized the opportunity to ask him one last thing. "Hey, you know, it's funny. My friends were under the impression that you're Spanish royalty or something. Are you?"

Juan laughed. "I'm not a prince, no. But I do come from a noble family. We're just a normal family, really. My parents and extended family own various businesses, and I'm working at my uncle's wine company, Rojas. Have you heard of it?"

"No, is it sold here?"

"Yes, wherever you can find wine."

"I'll look for it next time. I'm glad the mystery's solved."

"I hope your friends won't be too disappointed," Juan said with a smile. "What about you? Why didn't I know that your last name was Damour?"

"I was also traveling incognito," said Clémence. "It was easier to be an artist and just not have to explain that I was anything more than who I was, you know? When I met you, I had just broken up with my ex, and I wanted to escape from being me."

Her ex, Mathieu, was a talented artist, and she always felt as if she was in his shadow. She didn't want to be known just for being an up-and-coming painter's girlfriend or the rich daughter of successful parents; she just wanted to be Clémence.

"I get it," said Juan. "You wanted to be normal."

"You don't think I'm normal?" she joked.

"Damour is huge, even internationally."

"Again, that's my parents. I don't want to take credit for that."

"Do they live in this neighborhood, too?"

"Yes, but they're away in Asia right now. I'm house-sitting for them before I get my own place. We opened new stores in Toyko and Hong Kong, so they're going back and forth between the two cities for the next few months. They also want to open one in Singapore."

"That should be fun for them. Well, Clémence Damour of the Damour patisseries, I have your number, and we'll schedule something soon. Nice talking to you. I'm so glad I could run into you and explain myself."

"It was good to see you, too. I'd love to meet Sophie sometime."

They gave each other kisses on the cheeks good-bye, and Clémence went back to work to finally make the perfect apple pie croissants.

Chapter 5

When Clémence returned home after work, Arthur came by with his brother Theo. At twenty-six, Theo was working on his MBA. He knew about Arthur and Clémence's relationship, and she'd met him on several occasions. Theo was a bit shorter than Arthur, but with a wider build. He had the same hair and eyes, while his face shape was rounder and his nose stronger.

"Want a glass of wine?" Clémence offered the boys.

"Yes, please," Theo said.

Arthur came with Clémence into the kitchen to help her uncork a bottle of white wine. It pleased her because Arthur was used to being waited on hand and foot by the staff in the Dubois house. She used to think he was lazy and spoiled rotten because the family employed a full-time chef, and one of their maids even went upstairs to clean his and Theo's small rooms on the top floor every Saturday morning.

Theo chugged down his wine as if it were beer. Arthur had told him how she'd met Carlos/Juan, and he came to tell her what he knew about him.

"His name is not Carlos but Juan," said Theo.

"I know that now." Clémence told them about her run-in with him earlier at Place d'Iena.

"Even still," Theo said. "This guy sounds like he has an excuse for everything. When I heard that he simply disappeared on you, I thought that it was strange, but not surprising. There's something up with this guy."

"What do you mean?"

"Juan claims to be from a noble family, but something about his demeanor just doesn't fit the picture."

"Maybe it's because he's Spanish," said Clémence. "You're not used to his way of speaking and his cultural behaviors."

"Theo also has a little crush on Sophie," Arthur said. "So naturally he's suspicious of her boyfriend."

Theo turned red. "I'm not jealous. Sophie and I have been friends for years, and I don't have a crush on her. I just don't want to see her bamboozled by some Spanish phony. He acts like he's playing the lead in some romantic movie, saying all these incredibly cheesy things all the time. I can't believe she's falling for it."

"He says he's in love with Sophie," Clémence said. "Maybe he's just trying really hard to impress her."

"You mean like how Arthur is with you?" Theo teased his brother, who punched him in the arm. "Ow!"

Clémence grinned at Arthur. "I think it's kind of sweet that Juan is trying. I know I thought he was a nice guy when I was traveling with him. A bit slick, but he never took advantage of us, and he was fun."

"I know Juan sounds like this great guy," said Theo. "But I'm telling you, something is off. I don't know what it is, but just keep your eyes open, Clémence. I will too. I know you're good at investigations and things like that. I'm not asking you to spy on him or anything, but if you ever get a chance to find out more about him, do it."

"Okay." Clémence sat back on the couch and surveyed Theo. He looked serious. He must've really liked Sophie, to get so worked up about her boyfriend. She had to admit that some of Juan's excuses were a bit questionable, but they weren't completely unbelievable. "Juan said he wanted Arthur and I to double-date with them one day, so we'll see. How long has Sophie been with him, anyway?"

"Only a few weeks. She came back from Spain two weeks ago, and he's already weaseled his way into living with her. Why doesn't he have his own apartment, if he's so loaded?"

Theo shook his head. He chugged the rest of his white wine and excused himself. "I'll leave you two alone for the evening. *Bonne soirée*."

"*Ciao*, Theo."

When he left, Clémence turned to Arthur. "Your brother is a bit intense."

"He's awfully romantic. He's in love with Sophie. Has been for years, but he's too afraid to admit it, even to himself. But it's obvious, right?"

"Totally," said Clémence. "I feel bad for him. Sophie and Juan sound like they're pretty taken with each other."

"Well, I told Theo to move on, but who knows. Sophie has a sister who looks like her, so maybe he can move on with her."

Clémence made a face. "That's a bit creepy. Sophie's taken, so just go with the sister?"

"What? I'm just being practical for Theo," Arthur joked.

"Well, what if I was totally into you, but you weren't available, so I went on to Theo? He does look like you."

Arthur thought about it for a second. "Okay, fine. But I swear, if you ever get together with Theo, there'll be another murder case open in Paris."

Clémence laughed. "God, I won't. The same goes for you. I'll tear you a new one if you do."

"Getting dirty, are we?"

Arthur pulled her in for a kiss.

It wasn't long before they took their kisses into the bedroom.

Chapter 6

Clémence packed up her things after her first art class. She wasn't sure how she felt yet about her abstract rendering of a pistachio macaron. Her inner perfectionism and classical art education made her want to turn it into a realistic portrait of the real Damour macaron, but Clémence told herself that she was in this class for a reason. She wanted to play with different techniques and find a style she was comfortable painting in. Since she was just getting out of her comfort zone, it might take some time to get used to her new experimental style.

Catia had been extremely encouraging. She'd put a few different brushes in Clémence's hand throughout the class, thicker brushes that make denser lines than she was used to, bold lines that were indelible.

Clémence planned on painting a series with different Damour desserts and pastries, and displaying them in the *salon de thé*. Her parents would probably support her. She hoped they would like them.

Ben, whom she was meeting along with Berenice for a drink after the class, had encouraged Clémence to hold her own exhibition in a little gallery in Belleville, but she figured showcasing in Damour would be a fun, low-pressure way to start. Right now, some professional photographs of their desserts were on the walls, so why not her paintings?

After leaving her canvas along the wall to dry with the other paintings from the class, Clémence said good-bye to her new classmates and headed down the stairs.

To her surprise, she ran into a friend who was coming up the stairs, someone she had seen only hours earlier.

"Sebastien? What are you doing here?"

Sebastien's eyes widened, surprise fully evident in his expression. "What are you doing here?"

"I'm here for my art class," Clémence replied.

"Oh." Sebastien tugged at the strap of his gym bag. His cheeks turned pink.

"Is this where you've been going to on Tuesdays and Thursdays? The big secret that Berenice has been trying to expose?"

Berenice always questioned what Sebastien got off to in his spare time. Sebastien was so secretive that even his sister didn't know much about his private life. But now that Clémence was standing before him, he couldn't avoid telling her.

Sebastien nodded. "You caught me."

"Are you here for a dance class?" Clémence asked.

"I might as well tell you, shouldn't I? You're good at solving mysteries."

Clémence chuckled. "Only if you want to, but we're going to be running into each other. What's the shame in dance anyhow? What are you doing, tap? Hip hop?"

Sebastien sighed. "I'm taking ballet."

"Really? Wow. I really wasn't expecting that."

"Beginner adult ballet classes," Sebastien admitted. "My girlfriend Maya convinced me to do it with her."

"A girlfriend, huh?" Clémence grinned mischievously. "Berenice is going to be upset when she finds out that I knew before she did. I'm on my way to see her now, actually."

Sebastien groaned. "Don't tell her. My relationship with Maya is pretty new, and I don't want my sister poking around, scaring her off with her endless questions and her nosiness."

"Okay, I won't tell, promise, but she is your sister."

"If it gets really serious with Maya, I'm sure they'll find out...eventually."

"Maybe at your wedding, right?" Clémence joked.

"Anyway, I just thought it would be fun to take ballet with her, as long as no one knows about it. She convinced me to try it with her."

"Oh, come on. There's no shame in doing ballet if you're a guy. Look at Benjamin Pied."

"That's what Maya says," said Sebastien. "Well, I gotta go."

"Hey, so does this mean I'll get to meet Maya soon?"

"Don't push your luck, Damour." Sebastien sighed. "I'm sure it'll be inevitable if you're coming here every Tuesday and Thursday."

Clémence flashed him a grin as she passed him on her way down the staircase. "Ciao."

That was another mystery solved. If Berenice knew, she wouldn't constantly be wondering whether Sebastien was up to no good. It was always the quiet ones who worried Berenice, because she never knew what they were thinking. As brother and sister, they were so different. The only thing they really had in common was their love of baking and working at Damour together.

Berenice and Ben were already sitting outside Café Aux Folies, a popular café in Belleville. Clémence arrived and gave them both bisous hello. The couple had been dating ever since Clémence introduced them at Ben's spoken word performance, where he did a reading of one of his poems. They were both energetic, fun, and good-humored people, so it wasn't a surprise that the two took to each other. Ben was from England, and Berenice's English had improved as a result in recent weeks. Ben's French accent was starting to improve, as well.

Clémence ordered a mint tea and filled them in on what she'd been working on in her new art class. She also told Ben about her idea of painting desserts and showcasing them at Damour.

"That could work," he said. "Brilliant, actually, because of the exposure you'll get. The clientele at Damour is amazing to begin with. They'll get a sense of your style and learn your name. Who knows who will come in to sit down for lunch and then inquire about your paintings on any given day?"

"That's true," said Berenice. "Maybe someone will scout you."

"We should throw a launch party there when it happens."

"I'm just trying to concentrate on producing my best work," said Clémence. "Let's not get too ahead of ourselves now. They're just paintings of desserts."

"When are you going to show us your work?" Ben asked.

"It's only my first class." Clémence laughed. "Soon, I promise."

"I'll hold you to that."

"I know I haven't been painting as much as I should, but there has been a lot going on. Now that all the drama seems to have stopped, I can finally take it easy and get some work done."

"Amen." Ben held up his wine glass, and they all clinked glasses, then drank up. "Berenice has been helping me with the second draft of my mystery novel."

"It's really quite good," said Berenice, "especially now that I've fixed it."

"When do I get to read it?" Clémence asked.

"I'll let you read it when you show me your paintings," said Ben.

"So that's the way it's going to be, huh? Fine. It could be as early as next week. I'll have a couple to show you by then, at least. I'm so glad that the string of murders in this city is over and I can get some work done."

Little did Clémence know that another catastrophe would require her amateur sleuthing skills by the end of the weekend.

Chapter 7

*A*s a new personal rule, Clémence forced herself to take the weekends off from working at Damour. While she loved being in the kitchen—the sweet smells, the friendly staff, the delicious food, the excitement of creation, not to mention working with some of her best friends—she had workaholic tendencies to break.

Unlike most jobs, creating new dessert flavors didn't feel like work. The flagship store at 4 Place du Trocadero was only a couple of minutes' walk from her apartment, so it was only natural for Clémence to drop in whenever she wanted. She hadn't taken Arthur in to meet the staff yet. If the staff and some of the regular customers started talking, it wouldn't be long before their parents found out.

Aside from dropping in on Saturday morning to check on what was happening at Damour, Clémence spent the rest of her weekend with Arthur and Miffy, and worked on her paintings.

On Monday morning, Clémence returned to work early, as if to compensate for all the fun she had during the weekend loafing around the city and enjoying its beauty while hand-in-hand with her new love. As soon as she stepped into the kitchen, however, the sight of one man drained the joy right out of her.

Standing by Sebastien and Berenice's worktable was Inspector Cyril St. Clair. His tall, thin frame loomed over her, and his green eyes dimmed as they met hers. Clémence and Cyril were mostly archnemeses. Although they had shown cooperation in the past when they were forced to work together to solve a murder case, the peace never lasted for long.

"*Bonjour*," Clémence greeted him tersely. Cyril's presence was never a good sign. He usually showed up to accuse her of murder or something equally insulting.

"I'm thrilled to see you, too." His voice dripped with sarcasm, as Clémence was used to by now.

Clémence ushered him to a corner. "What is it this time? Don't tell me there's been another murder."

"You'd like that, wouldn't you?" Cyril's lips curled into a cruel smile, framed by deep lines in the shape of parentheses. "It would give Damour an edge: the patisserie for murderers and psychopaths."

Clémence sighed. "It's early Monday morning. I don't have time for patisserie murder jokes. Do you want something?"

"As a matter of fact, I'm on a missing person's case. Sophie Seydoux, do you know her?"

Her face fell. "Sophie is missing?"

"Yes. Now answer the question."

"Well, not directly, but I know people who do. We're in the same social circle. What happened?"

"She has been missing since Friday. She missed a family dinner yesterday, and her family thought perhaps she'd gone on a trip with her boyfriend for the weekend."

"How do you know she's not?"

"She's unreachable. Her phone is now shut off. However, her sister Madeleine received a text message from her boyfriend's cell phone yesterday evening. We have reason to believe that Sophie has been kidnapped."

"*Kidnapped?* What did the message say?"

"It was an incomplete message." He showed her a printout.

Help M, It's S. I've been taken. Dunno where I am. I'm all alone—

"She hasn't sent another message since," said Cyril. "It's highly probable that her kidnappers caught her sending the message and took the phone away. The phone's now disconnected."

"Or maybe they let her send the message on purpose. Kidnappers wouldn't let their victims play around with a phone, unless they were really careless and inexperienced."

"Are you a kidnapping expert, now?" Cyril sneered.

"Why are you here?" she demanded.

"Take a wild guess."

"I don't have time for games."

"I hear you know Sophie's boyfriend, Juan Camondo."

"Sort of. I just saw him last week." She told him everything she knew about Juan/Carlos, from how they met two years ago, to the conversation she had with him on the bench at Place d'Iena.

"We don't have any pictures of this guy. Sophie's sister says his name is Juan Camondo, but so far we haven't been able to match anybody by that name to how they've described him. There are plenty of Juan Camondos, but none with a face that any of her friends or family members recognize. The guy doesn't exist on record. The name is fake. He's a professional liar, and he's good. He must be dangerous."

Clémence gulped. Theo was right. There was something strange about Juan, but she'd never expected him to be a kidnapper. She had wanted to believe Juan/Carlos and all the excuses he gave about ditching her two years ago, but it seemed obvious now that he'd given Sophie and Clémence different fake names, and he only came to her to explain himself because he didn't want Clémence messing up his web of lies.

"He claims that his uncle is the founder of Rojas Wine," she said.

"We looked into that. The company was founded by an Australian couple who are expats in Spain. Another blatant lie. Do you know anything else about him?"

"Other than what I already've told you?" She racked her brain. "Well, he and Sophie were here at Damour eating crêpes last Tuesday afternoon, around four p.m. He paid by cash, though, so we couldn't trace his identity through a credit card, unfortunately. But we do have video surveillance at the store."

"You do? I never noticed any cameras."

Clémence walked him out to the salon, which was only half full since it was still early. Customers were drinking coffee, reading the papers, and eating breakfast.

"You see those chandeliers?" She pointed up at the two crystal chandeliers hanging from the lavender and gold-trimmed ceiling. "The cameras are hidden in there. Our surveillance company is located in the Fifteenth."

"Where were Sophie and Juan sitting at the time?"

Clémence walked over to the free table that the young couple had occupied. She sat in Juan's spot.

"You're lucky," she said to Cyril. "He was directly facing one of the cameras. I'd say it's more than likely that he'd been clearly captured on video."

"Good. For the first time I'm glad to step foot in this place. This guy slithers like a snake. He's extra good at avoiding video surveillance. None of Sophie's friends or family members have a picture of this guy. Since he thought this salon was surveillance-free, he might've felt safe enough to take one of his victims here."

"One of his victims?" Clémence whirled her head at him in shock. "He did this to others?"

"I have a theory," he said in his pompous voice. "Before I confirm it, I want to see his face. Where is this surveillance company?"

"I'll go with you," Clémence offered.

"I don't think it's necessary, Damour."

"I insist."

"Absolutely not."

"Look, if this Juan guy is as serious of a threat as you claim he is, I can help, since I've met him."

"Fine," Cyril said. "If I take you, you need to get me in touch with your friend Emily, to hear her side of the story."

"Sure. It's a deal. Let's go."

"I'm parked outside."

Cyril's tiny car was parked right in front of the store, but since the street was a busy roundabout, he had trouble getting out of his spot.

"*Merde*," he exclaimed. "Driving in this city, *c'est impossible.*"

Clémence had ridden in Cyril's car once, so she knew what she was in for. He was not only a horrible driver but an aggressive one, too. Drivers like him were the reason why Clémence never ever drove in the city. The Métro, as cramped and full of pickpockets as it was, or the odd taxi, in dire situations, suited her just fine.

"*T'es con, hein?*" Cyril shouted at one driver who cut in front of him. "Idiot!"

"Calm down!" Clémence exclaimed. "You're gonna get us killed!"

"This is how we drive in Paris, *mademoiselle*. If you don't fight for your place on the road, you get slaughtered."

Clémence sighed. Even though he'd been relatively friendlier during this visit, she simply didn't think much of Cyril St. Clair as a person. How he ever got to be a top inspector was a total mystery. The only thing he was ever right about was how driving in Paris was impossible. Some of the streets were simply too narrow, and there were other vehicles crowding the streets: motorcycles, mopeds, bikes—and those inexperienced tourist bikers on Vélibs, the rental bikes readily available around the city that merely cost a few euros to rent.

Fortunately, they only had to go one arrondissement over, to the 15th. Clémence directed him to the right address, and they found themselves in front of an inconspicuous storefront with no signage and darkly tinted windows.

Clémence knocked. "Ralph?" Nobody answered.

She tried the doorbell, which did the trick.

A scruffy-haired, scruffy-faced guy in his early thirties poked his head out.

"Oh. *Bonjour*," he said sheepishly. "Clémence. It's been a while."

Cyril introduced himself with so much self-importance that Clémence couldn't suppress rolling her eyes. Realizing he was in the presence of an inspector, Ralph Lemoine looked a bit nervous. He apologized for his attire, which was a Sex Pistols T-shirt, ripped jeans, and black Converse sneakers. Since he worked with a team of equally schlubby-looking guys, the work place didn't have a dress code. The office itself was really a converted apartment. Upon entering, they were in the kitchen, the sink of which was already piled with dirty dishes and espresso cups.

The rest of the team worked on the second floor, accessible by the staircase behind the wall where the fridge was. Ralph asked them whether they wanted anything to drink, which they both politely declined.

"We're looking for footage of a man in the Damour *salon de thé* in the 16th arrondissement location," Cyril said.

"Sure," Ralph said. He sat down in front of one of the many monitors crowding a long worktable, and punched on a keyboard. "For what date and time?"

"Tuesday at around four p.m.," Clémence said.

Ralph typed again. Two screens from the *salon de thé* chandelier cameras showed what was happening at the moment in real time. Clémence saw the waiters, some regular customers, and Caroline, the manager that day, on the screens.

"Do you know which camera you want to find the footage from?" Ralph asked.

"This guy was sitting here." Clémence pointed to one table shown on the left screen.

"That's camera two," Ralph said.

After a moment of fiddling, he retrieved the footage from the date and time Clémence requested.

"There he is," said Clémence.

Although the camera caught him from a high angle and his chin was cut off by the top of Sophie's head, they were able to see his face clearly.

Cyril smiled triumphantly. "*Bien.*"

"Is he a criminal?" Ralph asked.

"A kidnapper," said Cyril. "I suspect he's the guy who attempted to kidnap an heiress in Austria almost two years ago. A year later, he succeeded in kidnapping a Swiss heiress. This Juan guy certainly fits the description from these two other cases. We have a blurry picture of him from street surveillance in Zurich, but nobody ever managed to pin anything on him. He's good. He's probably working with a skilled team. Now that we have his picture, and proof of his connection with Sophie, plus witnesses—including you, Clémence—once we get this guy, we'll cream him."

"How are you going to catch him?" said Clémence. "Any clue where he is?"

"I'll be working with top investigators from Austria and Switzerland, and together, we'll find out this guy's real identity. I'm confident we'll get him."

"Fine, but what about Sophie?" she asked. "What are they going to do with her? What about the previous victims? Were they okay?"

"They're alive," said Cyril. "The Swiss heiress had been beaten, and bruises were found on her body."

"Geez." Ralph shook his head. "When did all these kidnappings start happening?"

"Like I said, two years ago. The first one with the Austria heiress didn't get pulled off as planned. The girl was lucky. A bodyguard managed to scare off the two kidnappers, clipping one of them in the arm with a gun when they tried to kidnap her in her home, but the men escaped. I think they aimed too high. The girl was practically Austrian royalty, fantastically rich. For the second target, they aimed a wee lower. Just some rich real estate mogul's daughter, but equally filthy rich. Juan was never caught, however, and he got away with millions. I'm sure it's the same guy. It can't be a coincidence that both girls had a boyfriend who fit Juan's description, and now there's a third victim with the same story."

"God." Ralph stared at the image of Juan frozen on the screen.

Clémence imagined Sophie being beaten, or worse. The realization dawned on her that Juan had probably traveled with them two years ago because he was scoping out whether they were worth kidnapping, and he'd left when he thought they weren't.

It could've been her. Clémence could've easily been the one kidnapped for ransom.

"Wow." Clémence sat down. Her head was dizzy with thoughts and fears of what could've been.

She'd never been so glad to have grown up middle-class. Just because Damour made them millionaires, wealth didn't change her. They lived in bigger apartments, had nicer clothes, and got to travel more, but Clémence was never ostentatious about her wealth. But had she given off a rich vibe when she met Juan? Perhaps. They had met in the bar of a five-star hotel, and all the girls had been dressed up in their finest clothes.

Emily's family was wealthy enough, but they weren't millionaires. After Juan found out how much she was worth, he probably moved on to Clémence. Then he dropped her too, after learning that her parents were bakers, not knowing that they founded the Damour patisseries.

"I want a screenshot of this man," Cyril told Ralph.

"Sure thing. I'll send it to your e-mail."

"Is there anything I can do?" Clémence asked.

"Not at the moment," Cyril said. "Although can you also send me the contacts of your friend Emily that you promised. I'd want to talk to her."

"Okay, but I want to help. I mean, what do you know about this guy? Where is he from, exactly? What was his upbringing like?"

"Look, Damour, you've done enough so far. Now if you want me to find Sophie as soon as possible, let me do my job." He headed out the door and then turned around before he closed it. "And don't forget to forward me Emily's contacts."

Cyril didn't even offer to drive her back.

Chapter 8

"Would you like a drink?" Ralph asked. "You look like you need one."

"Maybe a glass of water, please," Clémence replied.

Ralph obliged, putting the glass before her on the kitchen counter.

"They'll find your friend. Like the inspector said, the last girl came back alive."

"But she was beaten. God, how could I be stupid enough to trust this guy and his lies?"

"How could you have known? Don't be too hard on yourself."

Ralph was looking at her with a certain tenderness. He was cute in his scruffy way, but she had a boyfriend. And the way he looked at her said that he was definitely interested.

Clémence drank the water, stood up, and smiled. "Thanks for all your help today, but I better be going."

"No problem. I'm here, if you ever need any help. I promise the next time you see me, I'll be in a suit and tie." He winked at her. "Just give me advance notice."

Clémence couldn't help but smile. "Sure thing."

Outside, the bright sun contrasted with her sense of doom. The first thing she did was call Arthur.

"*Coucou, cherié*," he answered. "What's up?"

She explained everything that she'd learned that morning. "Did you know about this?"

"No. I don't think Theo knows, either. He's going to be really upset when I tell him."

"Cyril won't tell me anything else about Juan's potential identity. I want to speak to Madeleine. Theo, too. Can we all get together to talk somewhere right now?"

"Of course. I still can't believe Sophie actually got kidnapped. I'll call Theo, and I'll call you back after we make the plans."

"Sophie's apartment is probably being searched for clues right now," she said. "But how about Madeleine's place, wherever she lives? I want to meet there if she agrees."

"Okay."

Clémence's headache got worse. Anger rose to her chest. Juan! She had to get this guy. What kind of slime would woo girls, toy with their hearts, and kidnap them for ransom? This was some psychopath.

She went inside a Monoprix to calm herself down. It was hot outside, and the store was air-conditioned, which cooled her a little. She couldn't think when she was angry or stressed out, so she had to relax. It was also almost lunchtime. She was hungry, so she grabbed a salad and a bottle of organic pineapple juice, and sat in the café section of the store.

After she took a few bites of the chicken salad, her stomach felt better. She was able to think more rationally. What did she know so far? The kidnappings started happening two years ago. The first attempt was on an Austrian heiress. While Cyril didn't give the details, he'd said enough. She took out her smartphone and typed "Austrian heiress kidnapping" in the search engine. Sure enough, a few newspaper articles appeared about the thwarted attempt.

One of Mia von Koromla's bodyguards was able to fend off two kidnappers in the heiress's estate late in the evening. Gunshots were fired, and one of the kidnappers was shot in the arm before both masked men fled the scene. Mia has now been taken to an undisclosed location. She has round-the-clock security.

The prime suspect is Mia von Koromla's boyfriend, Victor Osuna, who claims to be from a noble Spanish family. After the kidnapping incident, Osuna disappeared without a trace. Police say he used a fake alias; his true identity has yet to be revealed...

Mia had dated him for three weeks. He had plenty of time to scope out her home, take pictures, and make note of the alarm systems. He was close enough to find out details such as the code to her alarm, the members of her security team, and when their shifts were.

The heiress, her family, friends, and members of her security team described Victor as suave, charming, and an all-round nice guy. They didn't want to believe that he could be the mastermind behind the kidnapping.

Clémence shook her head. Juan must've done the same to Sophie. He even managed to move into her apartment after a few weeks of dating.

Before she could Google the Swiss heiress, Arthur called her back.

"Okay, Theo and Madeleine are both at Madeleine's apartment right now. She lives in the Eighth, near Parc Monceau. Theo texted me her address with the door code, so I'll forward that to you."

"Great," Clémence replied. "I'll be there as soon as I can."

While traffic was always a challenge in the city, the morning rush hour had died down, and Clémence managed to flag down a cab. She told the driver to go in the direction of Parc Monceau until she received Arthur's text and was able to relay the exact address.

The area around Parc Monceau was full of rich jet-setters and celebrities. It suited socialites like Sophie and Madeleine Seydoux. The residents weren't as old and posh as the ones in the 16th, but it was still an exclusive neighborhood. While it wasn't as beautiful and expensive as the 6th arron-dissement, or artsy and charming like Montmartre, residents of the 8th arrondissement didn't have to put up with too many tourists, either. Not even in Parc Monceau, where it was packed with local kids under the care of full-time nannies. Many of the kids were the offspring of the rich and famous.

Clémence got out of the cab in front of 28 Boulevard de Courcelles. She punched in the entry code and pushed open the door, which took her into an elegant foyer. It had a small elevator barely big enough for two people, not unlike the elevator in her own building.

She went up to the sixth floor and rang the doorbell. Arthur answered. He greeted her with a kiss.

Madeleine introduced herself with a bright smile, although there was a look of worry behind her eyes. She had the same precious face and big brown doe eyes as her sister, except her hair was a lighter brown and it came down to her waist. She was also a well-known socialite in the Paris scene.

"Clémence, I'm sure I've met you before, years ago at one of those parties."

"*Oui*," Clémence replied. "I think we've met, too. I used to go to more parties, back in the day."

"Come on in. Would you like some wine?"

"Yes, please." Clémence did need a drink.

Theo stood up to greet her as well. He had dark circles under his eyes, his hair was a mess, and his navy tie was loosened around his neck.

Madeleine lived alone in the apartment, which was a luxurious but modest one bedroom. She explained that Sophie lived in the building across the street, and their parents' place, an apartment occupying two floors of a building, was right next to Parc Monceau. The Seydoux family wanted to stay living in the same area because they were all very close.

"I'm sorry this happened to your sister," said Clémence. She sat down on the couch and carefully placed her wine glass on the glass coffee table. The white rug underneath tempted stains of all kinds.

Madeleine's calm façade dropped; she looked down in sorrow. "I wish there was something

I could've done. I pray every day that she's not hurt and that it's just the money they want. If they contact us soon, we'll give them the money, no problem." She looked up at Clémence. "But I hear you're good at solving crimes. Maybe better than the police. Can you help us? My parents are devastated."

At the sight of Madeleine's sad face, Clémence's heart went out to her. What if it had been her own sister who was kidnapped for ransom? She couldn't imagine what that must feel like.

"I'm going to do all that I can. Tell me everything. Start with how Sophie met Juan."

"Sophie went to visit her friend Maria in Spain last month, during the long weekend. I couldn't go with her because my boyfriend Henri invited me to Provence. If I went, could I have prevented all this from happening? Changed her fate somehow?" Madeleine let out a long sigh. "Anyway, Sophie went to Seville, which is like a dream. She went out with Maria and some other girlfriends one night and met Juan at a bar. A couple of days later, she called home to say that she was staying in Spain for another week. She stayed with Juan in his hotel. It was truly a whirlwind romance. And then she extended her stay another week. When she came back to Paris, Juan came with her."

Theo's face darkened. "I knew this guy was trouble the moment I laid eyes on him. There was just something so fake about him."

"Unfortunately, I fell for his act," Madeleine admitted. "He was handsome, he had this cute accent, and he was so well dressed. He talked the talk. I thought, no wonder Sophie was mad for the boy. They moved into Sophie's apartment, and I met Juan for dinner on the first night. He asked a lot of questions about us. I thought he was the best listener I'd ever met, but little did I know he was just getting information about us for his kidnapping ploy!" She shook her head in anger. "The stuff he told us about his family were all lies. The loving way he treated Sophie—I really bought it. What an act!"

"He also told me he was madly in love with Sophie," said Clémence. She told Madeleine about how she'd seen Juan eating crêpes with Sophie at Damour, and how he'd run into her on the street the day after, when he explained why he was in Paris. "Now I realize he just wanted me to be on his good side so I wouldn't blow his cover to Sophie. I wonder if he followed me around just so he could pretend to run into me."

"I'd say it's more than likely," said Theo.

Arthur had already filled Theo in on how Clémence originally met Juan two years ago, but

Madeleine had more questions. "Did Juan tell you that he was from Madrid?"

"Yes, but he was insinuating that he was Spanish royalty. That was two years ago, before the Austrian heiress kidnapping attempt. I think he has perfected his lies since then. He got close with Mia von Koromla; he was able to successfully kidnap a Swiss heiress a year later."

"The inspector didn't tell us that. Who is this Swiss girl?"

Clémence didn't know, either, but she performed the Google search for the kidnapping. She scrolled through the articles and found one to read out loud.

"Livia Egle, the kidnapped heiress who had been held ransom for four million euros, was released in the middle of the woods in western Switzerland yesterday. She is currently hospitalized for trauma. No physical injuries have been reported. She was held captive for nine days.

"A ransom call was placed on the Egle family on the evening of her kidnapping for the four million sum. A man by the name of Don Alba is the prime suspect. Egle's former boyfriend, he disappeared around the time the victim was kidnapped and hasn't been heard from since. Police are still searching for him."

"This was last year?" Madeleine asked.

Clémence nodded. "On May twenty-eighth. Looks like our Juan, or whatever his name is, wants to make this an annual project. The inspector has a decent photograph of him now for his investigation."

She explained how the photo came from a freeze-frame of his face from store surveillance.

"It makes sense now why he's so camera-shy," said Madeleine. "When I asked Sophie to send me pictures of Juan, she couldn't because she said Juan didn't like having his picture taken. He claimed he had an aversion to the paparazzi ever since he was a child and wanted utter privacy, so Sophie respected it."

"I'm hoping Inspector St. Clair knows what he's doing this time," Arthur said.

"He's working with the police from Austria and Switzerland to find out Juan's real identity," Clémence added.

"But will it be too late?" Madeleine moaned. "Why haven't they called us yet?"

"I bet Juan's a real nobody," said Theo. "No wonder he's so under the radar."

Clémence nodded. "Like he told me once, he's just an average guy. Just a guy using his good looks and charm to make a buck off his rich victims. He's pretty good. He really studied the behaviors of the rich. Not that I'm an expert on upper-class society, but he had me fooled."

"He had us all fooled," said Madeleine. "I wonder what's taking so long for him to contact us. Sophie has been gone since the weekend. At first, I didn't think much of it when she didn't return my texts, because she was so wrapped up with Juan. He was all she talked about. When she missed family dinner, we all speculated whether she went off on an impromptu weekend trip away with him. Then I got the text and had to call the police."

"Yes, Cyril told me about that. I wish she was able to write more to tell us where she was."

Tears welled in Madeleine's eyes. "The inspector said she probably couldn't finish her text because her kidnappers took the phone away—Juan's phone. Do you think he punished her for that? I just want her back. We'll pay the ransom. Why don't they just call?"

Clémence put a hand over hers. "Let's figure out what we can. I do think it's a bit odd that they haven't called your family for ransom yet, since the article said they had called the Egle family on the same night, but maybe they will later today. In the meantime, we need to find out more about Juan and the whole kidnapping procedure. I want to get in touch with Livia Egle. She's the only one who lived through this whole ordeal. She must be able to provide us with some valuable information."

"Okay." Madeleine stood up and went to look outside the window. She gripped her cell phone in her hand as she stared out onto the street below. "I must know somebody in my social circle who can put me in touch with her. I'm going to make a few calls."

Chapter 9

Clémence left Madeleine to make the calls to her friends. She went back to her apartment alone, where Miffy greeted her excitedly since she'd been out of the house longer than usual. usually went home for lunch to take care of her little white highland terrier. Miffy was her parents' dog. Since she was house-sitting for them, she was also the dog-sitter. Miffy was the most cheerful dog Clémence ever had the pleasure of knowing, and the sight of the little white dog boosted her spirits immediately.

She forwarded Emily's contacts to Cyril on her phone. On the way home, she'd talked to Emily herself, but Emily didn't tell her anything new that Clémence didn't know already.

Disappointed by the lack of clues, she made herself a shot of espresso in the kitchen. She sat down at the breakfast table, with a notebook and pen, and wrote down everything she knew about Juan and the kidnapping case so far. It didn't help her gain any new insights as to who Juan was and where he might've taken Sophie, but she felt better to write it all down. It made her feel as if she was doing something when there was nothing much she could do at the moment. All the different names and lies that Juan used were confusing, and it might come in handy to keep them straight.

She wondered what kind of story he had told Livia Egle. Was it really that easy for a man to make a girl fall in love? Was love real if it only one person felt it and the other was faking it?

Poor Sophie. Not only must she be scared out of her mind in her hostage situation, she was probably also sad and heartbroken. Clémence couldn't imagine what she must be going through.

Clémence felt as helpless as Madeleine, not knowing which step to take next in finding Sophie. Only Cyril would have the resources to uncover Juan's identity, but would that even help? Even if they found out who he was, how would they know where Juan had taken her? The cell phone was now off, making it untrackable. They could be in Paris, it could be in another city or town in France, or it could be in another country altogether. Her main hope at this point was to talk to the Swiss heiress. Maybe there were some patterns from Juan's behavior and tactics in that hostage situation that could point her in the right direction.

On a separate page, she prepared a list of questions she wanted to ask Livia. The heiress had not given any interviews to the media about what had happened. Instead, she had avoided the spotlight for months. It must've been a painful topic for her. Clémence didn't want to cause Livia further pain with her questions, but they needed to be asked.

She did some more research on Livia on the Internet. She read through all the kidnapping articles, as well as old interviews that revealed more about Livia's personal life.

Livia Egle was the heiress of her father's real estate company. She had been a popular socialite and It girl, often traveling to New York and Paris to keep up with the fashion scene, until the kidnapping incident. After she was released, she became averse to the camera.

She still had her high-end jewelry line, which was well received on both sides of the pond. Now thirty, she lived a more grounded life, designing jewelry behind the scenes and traveling around the world with her tech entrepreneur boyfriend. There were still some recent paparazzi shots of the heiress, but she was always wearing sunglasses and never smiled anymore.

This was in contrast to the old Livia, pre-kidnapping, when she used to happily step out to red carpet events and pose for the cameras with the eagerness of a girl on the verge of becoming the next big thing.

As Clémence looked through photos of the icy blonde, who bore a resemblance to Grace Kelly, she noticed the gorgeous dresses she used to wear. No wonder Livia was considered to be a fashion icon. Several of the gowns and party dresses were made in the same flowy style, in muted colors, and designed by someone she'd never heard of: Marcus Savin.

Clémence read one of her old interviews from an online fashion magazine, where Livia talked about how her favorite designer was this Marcus Savin. He was a designer friend whose work she was obsessed with.

The designer's last name was French, and after Googling him, Clémence found out that not only was he from Paris, he had a store not far from where she lived, on Avenue Montaigne. She wondered if the designer knew Livia, and whether he could help her get in touch with her.

As she began dialing the number for the Marcus Savin store, Madeleine called her. She told her that she did manage to contact a friend who knew Livia.

"Where is Livia right now?" Clémence asked. "Did you find out?"

"She's on a plane back to Switzerland from Russia. But get this—she's planning on coming to Paris tomorrow evening for a private party. Apparently her family sponsored the Royal Jewels exhibit at the Grand Palais. She rarely makes appearances at big events, so we'll be able to talk to her in person. That is, if I can score invitations to this party."

"Wait, the party is at the Grand Palais?"

"Yes. For one evening only. It's by invitation only, for special guests. I wonder why I wasn't on the list. But no matter. I'll make some more calls, and I'm sure I can get us in."

"But can't we talk to her before then? Tomorrow's a bit late. Can we get in touch with her by phone or Skype today?"

"I'll try, Clémence, but my friend Laura says Livia's busy traveling. Laura can't even get hold of her at the moment. All she knows is that Livia's going to be at this party."

"Okay." Clémence was disappointed.

"But I'll try harder," Madeleine insisted. "I'm calling more friends to see if anyone else knows her and can reach her."

"Thanks, Madeleine."

By the time Clémence started on dinner, Madeleine called back with good news and bad news. The good news was that she'd scored invitations for the four of them. The bad news was that Livia was still hard to reach. Since she was on a long flight back from Russia, her phone didn't have a good connection.

Their best bet to talk to her was to go to the party. Livia might not have a spare moment tomorrow, either, because she might be jet-lagged and taking another flight from Switzerland to Paris.

Arthur dropped by after dinner. He was obliged to dine with his family because one of his brothers had done well on his exams. Clémence invited him to the party at the Grand Palais as her date, and he accepted.

They discussed the case a bit, but it wasn't long before they were talking in circles. Ultimately, there was nothing much they could do until they spoke to the heiress.

"Maybe by tomorrow, something will have happened," Arthur said. "The Seydoux might finally get the ransom call, or the police might find Juan's identity or even a location. There's nothing we can do, so let's relax for the evening."

"You're so sensible." Clémence kissed him on the forehead.

Arthur and Clémence had shared a bed the previous night, and he seemed keen on spending another evening there as well. Was he planning to make it a habit?

She didn't mind. More than didn't mind. She used to think that dating a neighbor was a bad idea, but now she realized how convenient it was.

Together in bed, he held her close, and she drifted off to sleep smelling his warm scent, with the lingering thought that she wouldn't mind if Arthur just moved in altogether...

In the middle of the night, a noise woke Clémence up. The walls of her building—in most French buildings for that matter—were as thin as Band-Aids. She was used to hearing creaks, thuds, and voices at all hours of the day, but something about this noise alerted her to consciousness. Had it been a door closing? Her own bedroom door?

"Arthur," she murmured. "Did you hear that?"

"Hmm?" Arthur's eyes remained closed.

Once her vision adjusted to the darkness, she noticed nothing unusual.

Until Miffy suddenly started barking. Loudly, with a kind of ferocity that she'd never heard from her parents' dog before.

Clémence shook Arthur awake. "Arthur, get up. Even Miffy's scared. I think there's someone here."

That got Arthur's attention. He got out of bed and tried to shake himself awake.

"I'll check," he whispered.

Arthur unplugged a lamp from one of the bedside tables and took the shade off. It was one of her mother's antiques, made out of brass. It was sturdy and long enough for Arthur to defend himself, should he need to.

Sometimes Clémence was creeped out about living alone in such a big apartment. There were three bedrooms and two bathrooms, plus an extra toilet in a small, closet-sized room with a tiny sink. While her parents' bedroom was next to the living room, she took one of the guest rooms, accessible through a long hallway.

They turned on the lights in the hallway, which revealed nothing unusual. The end of the hallway led them to the front door.

Miffy had calmed down at this point, and at the sight of them, she ran to her. Clémence wanted to hug her, but she had to keep her arms free in case she needed to defend herself.

Ready for action, Arthur checked the main bedroom, including its bathroom and the connected walk-in closet. He checked the living room, the office, and the kitchen. At Clémence's insistence, he also went back to the hallway to check the other guest bedroom.

Nothing.

"Everything seems normal," Arthur announced. "Do you see anything missing?"

"No," Clémence said. All of her mother's jewelry was in her box. The valuable artwork and antiques were all in their place. "But do you smell that?"

It was faint, but there was a hint of something in the air. An oak moss smell.

"I think it's men's cologne."

"Maybe." Arthur sniffed. "It's not very strong, but I smell it, too."

"Someone was definitely here."

Clémence turned the knob of their front door. It opened easily. At night, Clémence locked the front door from the inside. The apartment had an alarm, but she only put it on when nobody was home. It wasn't convenient to put on the alarm at night. She would set it off as soon as she passed one of the alarms, and she wouldn't be able to walk freely around the apartment.

"So someone broke in," said Arthur. He looked at the lock from the front of the door. "These are pros. The lock doesn't look too tampered with. Are you sure you locked it tonight?"

"Positive."

Clémence called the police, then she called her security company, letting them know of a break-in.

"Do you think this has anything to do with Juan?" Clémence said, her eyes wide. "He's still out there, and he's kidnapped one heiress."

Arthur went silent for a moment. His eyes darkened. "I'd say there's a pretty good chance."

"What if their plan was to kidnap me tonight? They might've even opened my bedroom door and saw me, because I heard a door close. Maybe they expected me to be alone but saw you, so they decided to abandon the attempt. Then Miffy started barking at them in the hallway and that scared them off. Oh my gosh. Good thing you were here with me."

Arthur pulled her in for a hug. "Don't worry. You're safe now. Whoever it was, they're gone. Maybe it was just a failed robbery attempt. It happens a lot in the Sixteenth."

"Sure, but it seems like too much of a coincidence. What if he wants to get me, too? Maybe that's why he hasn't contacted the Seydoux family for ransom money yet. He planned on kidnapping me, too."

Chapter 10

The police showed up. With no evidence and no witnesses other than Miffy, all they did was file a report. Their *gardien*, the caretaker of the building, whose own apartment was situated near the front door of the building, hadn't seen or heard anything unusual, either.

Clémence didn't give up so easily. She called Inspector Cyril St. Clair in the middle of the night and told him her theory that she'd been the target of a kidnapping attempt.

In the past Cyril might have written her off, but due to her string of successes in solving murder cases, he begrudgingly gave her the benefit of the doubt.

The next morning, Cyril came over with four members of his forensics team.

"Your damn dog probably ruined a lot of the DNA evidence on the floor," Cyril complained. "Keep her contained."

Miffy was already in her arms. Clémence sighed. She hadn't had a lot of sleep, and she didn't want to start another argument with Cyril so early in the morning. She had been planning on asking Madame Dubois to keep Miffy until Cyril's team was finished, anyway.

Most of her neighbors, including the Dubois family on the third floor, heard about the break-in. Unfortunately, this also prompted Arthur to reveal to his family than he had been with Clémence during the night because they were dating.

Madam Dubois was thrilled. She'd wanted her eldest son to go out with Clémencc for some time, and she felt proud, as if she was responsible for making it happen.

When she answered the door, looking chic as usual in a powder blue Chanel jacket and skirt set, she began gushing over how thrilled she was about Arthur and Clémence being an item.

Clémence blushed and thanked her. It was funny how Madame Dubois was more interested in their budding romance rather than the break-in.

Arthur came to his mother's side. "*Maman*, you're embarrassing Clémence."

Miffy ran into the living room to play with Youki, a Jack Russell terrier belonging to the Dubois family.

"I'm just happy that my son's actually dating someone wonderful for a change. Oh, and it's a pity about the robbery attempt. I know how horrible that feels." Madame Dubois had been robbed before.

The family also owned an estate in Honfleur, which wasn't in use for most of the year. Four years ago, the thieves had taken off with precious paintings that had been in the family for years.

"It wasn't a robbery," said Arthur. "It was a kidnapping attempt."

"Oh, a kidnapping. Right. The point is to be careful. I'd get a bodyguard if I were you, Clémence."

"I think I'm all right for now," said Clémence. "The police are going to keep an eye on the building for the next little while."

"And I'll be by her side," Arthur said.

Dubois beamed proudly at her son. Arthur used to date all sorts of girls that his mother didn't approve of, and Clémence must've seemed like a saint in comparison. Clémence was glad to have her approval, and it wasn't going to be long before her own parents learned about their relationship.

That cemented it. Clémence and Arthur were officially a couple.

Clémence excused herself to go back up to her apartment. Arthur walked her up.

"The kidnappers probably won't attempt anything in the daytime, anyway," said Arthur. "Too many people are coming and going on the streets and in this building. But as soon as it gets dark, you're sticking with me, Clémence. Why don't you come sleep in my room on the roof tonight?"

Since the rooms on the top floor were so small, there must've been at least seven other tenants living up there, including Ben. Kidnappers wouldn't be able to walk down the hall without their footsteps attracting attention. Even if they were successful, their escape would be difficult, as they would have to run down seven flights of stairs.

"It's not a bad idea," said Clémence, "but isn't it a bit small for the two of us?"

"It's not small. It's cozy."

Clémence laughed. "Fine. We'll pretend we're camping in a tent."

Arthur needed to finish some work at the library, and he kissed her good-bye. "Stay away from dark alleys."

"I will."

"Seriously. I'll be home before it gets dark."

Back in her apartment, Cyril's forensics team was still busy gathering evidence. Clémence didn't know whether it was fortunate or unfortunate that she wasn't able to get a glimpse of her midnight intruders. Maybe they had guns on them or brought rope to tie her with. She shuddered at the thought.

She wanted to do something useful, like work at Damour, but she knew she would be too distracted to do a good job. Instead she hung around at home, anxious to see if the team would find anything.

"So Cyril, anything new on the kidnapper?" she asked.

Cyril crossed his arms. His nostrils flared and his eyes rolled. His bad humor was even more evident in the early morning.

"Not yet, Damour."

"Really? I thought you said you were confident you would be able to find out Juan's real identity."

Cyril lost his temper. "Damour, we're trying to do our job. Will you just leave us alone? I can't do anything with you breathing down my neck."

Clémence didn't like to be yelled at, naturally, but she knew Cyril had a point. She wasn't helping much sticking around and asking questions. She decided to take a walk outside for some fresh air.

As she made her way to Place du Trocadéro, Madeleine called her.

"Clémence! Are you okay? Theo told me someone broke into your apartment last night. It must've been so frightening!"

"I'm okay, Madeleine. Nobody's hurt."

"I've been paranoid myself, but now it looks like it's for good reason."

"I really didn't expect it," Clémence said. "They already have one girl. I think they're getting pretty greedy with two."

"A double-kidnapping," Madeleine remarked. "We should all be careful. I'm staying with my boyfriend Henri tonight. I doubt they'd want to kidnap me, too, but you never know."

"Right. It has to be Juan. It wouldn't be hard for him or anyone on his team to have figured out where I live. It's so creepy to think that someone followed me home and devised a plan to try to take me in the night. I guess that's why they haven't made the ransom call to your family yet. They wanted to wait to get me."

"I feel so helpless," said Madeleine. "What can we do?"

"We're going to this party to meet Livia tonight. It's the only thing we can do for now. What time should we meet?"

"Let's go early in case Livia gets there early. The invite says eight p.m., but we can try seven forty-five."

"Sure."

"It's going to be a big event with lots of important people. Anyone who's anyone is going to be there. It turns out that some of my friends are going, too. I can't believe I didn't get an invite without having to ask! Sophie would kill to come—" Madeleine stopped. "I miss Sophie. I hope she's okay."

"Don't worry. We'll get to the bottom of this tonight," Clémence reassured her, even though she wasn't one hundred percent confident.

"My parents are extremely stressed. Did the inspector tell you what he was able to find so far? He wouldn't tell us anything."

Clémence bit her lip. She was tempted to complain about Cyril's incompetence and how they didn't find out much so far, but she didn't because Madeleine was in enough pain already.

"He's doing his best," Clémence replied. "Who knows, maybe he will find some DNA or clues or something from my house. Let's try to stay optimistic."

"Okay, well, I'll see you at the party tonight. It's not very fashionable to be early, but who cares about keeping up appearances at this point? Oh, and it's a black-tie event. Do you have something to wear?"

"Good question," said Clémence.

"If you don't, I'd be happy to lend you something. Although I've been photographed in most of my dresses. We'll probably be photographed tonight as well."

"Thanks. That's very sweet. Maybe it's best to buy something." She thought about the Marcus Savin store. "I think I'll head down to Avenue Montaigne and do some shopping to unwind. If I don't find something, I'll take you up on your offer."

"Yes, shopping's a great stress reliever. Oh, what about makeup and hair? Who's doing it for you?"

"I am."

"Darling, it's best to get a pro, and I have a couple of people coming by my house to do my hair and makeup tonight. Why don't you come to my house before six tonight so we can get our hair and makeup done together?"

"Sure," said Clémence.

Chapter 11

Clémence didn't have to go home and look inside her closet to know that she didn't have anything for a black-tie event. She hadn't updated her wardrobe in the two years that she'd been gone, and the gowns she did own, she had been photographed in, as well. She understood Madeleine's caution. If she wore one of them again, the tabloids would surely criticize her for recycling old dresses.

As funny as it sounded, she needed to buy a new dress to avoid media attention. If she wore a decent dress, they'd feature her in a fashion or gossip blog or two, instead of ripping her apart for bad taste or wearing an out-of-style dress. Blending in meant having to look as good as the other guests. Like Madeleine, there were going to be well-known and well-respected people at this party, everyone from media moguls and celebrities to designers and socialites such as herself. She didn't know what else she could be categorized as, other than a socialite, as much as she detested the term. In the scheme of things, she was a nobody.

It was silly to be worrying about what she would be wearing to a party, given the circumstances, but she couldn't help but feel nervous about going to one of these events again, especially after she'd avoided them for so long.

She wondered if her ex-boyfriend Mathieu would be there. He used to love going to events with her. He was a bit of a social climber, and being part of the scene made him feel important and glamorous. Now that he was a little more well known for his art and a regular fixture on the Paris social scene, maybe he was starting to receive these invitations on his own. She had long gotten over him, but she still hoped she never had to see his face again.

Sometimes she did have fun and met all kinds of interesting people at these types of events, and this party sounded like one of the better ones. It was at the Grand Palais, of all places. But this time she wasn't there to party and be photographed like some wannabe It girl. Keeping up appearances used to cause her much more anxiety, but avoiding criticisms from the media (i.e., catty blog posts and tweets) were only of minor importance now. She had bigger things to worry about, like finding out who the kidnappers were, where they had taken Sophie, and how to avoid being kidnapped herself.

She went downstairs and walked to Avenue Montaigne where all the high-fashion stores were, including Marcus Savin's. With all the chaos happening around her—and to her—recently, she thought it would be a refreshing break to look at some designer gowns. She hadn't gone clothes shopping in ages.

As she passed five-star hotels, fancy restaurants, and wealthy locals and visitors on the street carrying bags from Chanel, Prada, and Louis Vuitton, she checked her phone and saw a missed call from Sebastien. They were supposed to be working on a couple of new recipes together, and she hadn't been in all morning. Clémence had to call back and explain again what had been going on lately. She simply wasn't in the right frame of mind to focus on inventing new dessert and pastry flavors when the kidnapping case was occupying one hundred percent of her thoughts.

While she was on her phone, she checked the address of the Marcus Savin shop. She would've passed the small store if she hadn't checked. It was right beside the Valentino store. Unlike the other high-end designer shops, the Marcus Savin storefront was not very flashy. There was a small sign, one window display, and that was it.

A beautiful lavender dress in the window caught her eye. It was made out of silk, in the same flowy Grecian goddess style that looked so flattering on Livia Egle. Savin's dresses looked even better in person, and Clémence had the primal urge to go in to take a closer look.

The dress probably cost an average person's annual salary, however. Her middle-class upbringing always made her hesitant about making extravagant purchases, even though she had the money. She pushed the door open. She could at least look at the gown, right?

"*Bonjour*," a beautiful blond saleswoman in her forties greeted her. "I saw you admiring the new gown at the window. It's gorgeous, isn't it?"

"Stunning," Clémence agreed. She turned to look at the back of the dress, and it was lovely from that angle too.

The dress had an open back, with the fabric meeting at a V at the waistline. The lavender silk was so delicate and pretty, while the cutouts at the sides of the waist gave it a modern edge.

"Do you want to try it on?" the woman asked.

Clémence bit her lip. She was supposed to look good enough to stay under the radar, but this dress was a showstopper. Maybe it wouldn't look as good on her, and there was no harm in trying it on. "Well, okay."

She surveyed Clémence's frame. "We have it in your size. Do you want to take a look around while I get the change room ready for you?"

"*Oui, merci.*"

"*Je m'appelle Vivien*. Ask me if you have any questions."

As she looked through the other dresses, including a pink minidress and a navy off-the-shoulder number, she was positive that she would walk away with something from Marcus Savin. How come she'd never heard of the talented designer before?

"How long has this store been here?" Clémence asked Vivien when she came back.

"Just a little over a year, although he opened his first store in New York four years ago. Marcus has been designing for over a decade. He's worked at Gucci and Chloe, but he started his own line five years ago, and it's been going strong since."

"He's certainly talented."

"This black dress would look good on you too." Vivien took out a more modest dress from the rack to show her. "What kind of party are you going to?"

"It's a black-tie event at the Grand Palais."

"Oh, Marcus Savin is going to that party tonight, as well."

"Really? I wanted to ask, is there a way to get in touch with Marcus?"

"What do you want to get in touch with him about?"

"It involves a mutual friend, Livia Egle. It's kind of personal but important."

"Well," Vivien considered. "Why don't you try on the dress first, and I'll see what I can do?"

Clémence obliged. She had a little trouble getting into the dress at first, because the zippers were hidden within the silk folds. She also had to be careful not to rip the dress, because it seemed so fragile. When she came out, she couldn't believe her reflection in the mirror. She twirled, trying to admire herself from all angles.

It wasn't that Clémence thought she was particularly beautiful; the dress was the spectacular one, and it seemed to be made for her. The lavender brought out the pink in her cheeks, livened up her pale skin, and was a flattering contrast to her dark sleek bob. The silk felt lovely on her skin, and it was draped over her five-foot-four frame, falling to the floor with just enough drama, but not so much length that she couldn't walk without tripping all over herself.

Somebody clapped behind her.

"Bravo. That's how this dress should be worn."

Clémence turned to face the male speaker. A dashing man in a charcoal suit and a blue bow tie walked down the staircase, following Vivien. He had a thin mustache above his lip, and his hair was dark and waxy, parted and neatly gelled like an old-fashioned movie star.

"Surprise. This is the designer himself," Vivien introduced, "Marcus Savin."

Clémence smiled brightly and shook the handsome man's hand. "You're very talented. Lovely to meet you. I'm Clémence Damour."

"Vivien tells me that you're going to the Grand Palais party tonight."

"Yes, I am."

"So am I." He examined her. "Are you somebody I'm supposed to know?"

"Er, I don't think so. Why?"

"Are you an actress?"

"*Moi?*" Clémence blushed. "No way."

"I thought you were an actress because you're too short to be a model. That's too bad, because I could use a girl like you to walk in my next show. It's a pity that the industry is so keen on using giraffes instead."

Clémence laughed. She liked Marcus already. There was something refreshing about his bluntness and dry humor. "No, I work at Damour. Have you heard of the patisseries?"

"Oh wait, you're Clémence Damour. Of course! I thought your face looked familiar. I think I've seen you in Paris Match once. I buy macarons from your store all the time, and I'm obsessed with your *pains au chocolat.*"

"Thank you."

"What happened to you? Didn't you used to go out with that artist guy, Mathieu something?"

"That was me. You know all this?"

"Sure, I keep tabs on who's who in this town. I see him in the papers sometimes, but not you. What happened?"

"Well, I was never big on the socialite scene. The only reason I'm going to the party tonight is to meet Livia Egle."

"Livia? I know her, although I haven't seen her in ages. I designed her wedding dress four years ago, although her marriage lasted less than all the time it took for me to make the darn dress! Why do you want to meet her?"

"Are you a close friend of hers?"

"Close? Well, I would've said so a few years ago. We're still friends now, and she has always been a great supporter of my brand, but she's also someone who dropped off the face of the earth last year, right after her, you know, unfortunate incident."

"The kidnapping?"

"Poor girl. Who could blame her, really? It must've been terrifying, but she refuses to talk about it."

"Do you know Sophie Seydoux?" asked Clémence.

"Yes, she's an acquaintance. I've dressed her before."

"Well, did you know that she's been kidnapped?"

Marcus gasped. "No. She has? Recently?"

Clémence nodded. "Allegedly by the same man who kidnapped Livia. It's why I want to talk to her. Can you please help me get in touch with her? I'm a friend of Sophie's family, and we want to find out more about the kidnapper and Livia's experiences with him."

"Okay, wow." Marcus thought about it for a moment. "I can try calling her now."

Marcus pulled out his cell phone and made the call, but he left what sounded like a voicemail message.

"Not there?"

"Led me straight to voicemail. Her phone must be turned off. She does that throughout the entire flight when she's flying, just in case. Her cousin died in a plane crash when she was young, so she gets paranoid about flying. If she calls back, I can give her your number."

"That would be great." Clémence wrote it down for him.

"My condolences to Sophie's family. When did this happen?"

"She went missing as early as Friday."

"I didn't know."

"It's not public knowledge yet. It's unfortunate because there's nothing much we can do."

Marcus nodded. "If she doesn't call back, I'll introduce you tonight. Tell me you're going in that dress."

"It's beautiful, but maybe *too* beautiful. Maybe I'll try on the black."

"Honey, the black would of course look great on you too, but my lavender dress is made for you. Tell you what. Why don't I let you borrow the dress for the night?"

"What? You don't have to do that."

"Yes, I insist. It's more for my business than for you. You're going to be photographed in the dress, and you're the perfect person to sell it. Trust me, it's more for my benefit than yours."

"Well..." Clémence examined herself in the dress again. She would be photographed, wouldn't she?

She had mixed feelings about being in the spotlight. People could be so cruel sometimes. She was never that famous, but Marcus was making it sound as if she was an A-lister who would be catapulting him to fame instead of the other way around. Still, the offer was tempting. If she bought the dress, it wasn't as if she would wear it again after she'd been photographed in it, and it would've been money wasted.

"Okay, I accept. Thank you so much, Marcus."

"No problem. Vivien will help you wrap up the dress at the cash. I'm sure you're going to be absolutely stunning. I'll see you tonight."

Chapter 12

The makeup artist finished working on Clémence's face as Madeleine got her hair done. Madeleine's long brown hair was in loose waves, and one side was pinned up with a diamond barrette. She wore a matching diamond necklace and a silver vintage Chanel dress.

Clémence's hair was a challenge to work into a style other than her current bob. The dress was gorgeous enough on its own, so the hair stylist only straightened her hair. Her makeup was kept simple and glowing.

Their dates had been ready long ago. Arthur and Henri were sitting in the living room, wearing dashing tuxedos, drinking beer, and watching a soccer game on TV.

When the girls stepped out from Madeleine's bedroom, the boys stood up. Madeleine's boyfriend Henri must've been used to seeing Madeleine all glammed up, because he only made a small comment about how pretty she was and turned back to the TV.

Arthur, on the other hand, couldn't stop staring.

"Cut it out," Clémence said, laughing.

"Wow, that dress on you… Wow."

Clémence blushed. "Come on. We're going to be late."

"Extremely early, you mean," Henri said.

Madeleine had a limousine drive the four of them to the Grand Palais.

The Grand Palais was an exhibition hall in the 8th arrondissement that hosted various art and photography exhibitions throughout the year. The architecture of the building was both classical and modern, with a stone facade and art nouveau ironwork. With its glass barrel-vaulted roof, the Grand Palais always reminded Clémence of a fancy and massive greenhouse.

When they pulled up behind a pile of other limos and cars, she could see the red carpet rolled out by the grand entrance, as well as the photographers who lined around it, behind the velvet rope.

"Have you ever been to this kind of thing?" Clémence asked Arthur.

"*Jamais*," said Arthur. "Never. I rarely get invited to these things, and when I do, I ignore them."

Clémence smiled. Arthur was a bit antisocial, but that was part of what she liked about him. He was the opposite of Mathieu, who needed to be the center of attention at all times.

They thought they were going to be early, but apparently they were right on time. The cameras were blinding, and Clémence tried to smile through it all. This was more overwhelming than any event she'd been to in the past. She was holding Arthur's hand very tightly. She couldn't tell whose hand was sweating more.

Arthur found it difficult to muster a smile for the cameras, despite the paparazzi telling him to do so. He wasn't the type to smile on command. When they walked up the stairs behind Madeleine and Henri into the front doors of the Grand Palais, she was relieved beyond words. She didn't know how real celebrities did it. They must've had to use extra-strong antiperspirants, too.

The inside was air conditioned, and she started to cool down. Livia's family had sponsored the "The Royal Jewels", an exhibit that featured extravagant jewelry from members of the royal family all across Europe.

The first thing that greeted them in the grand hall was a striking piece of modern art: a giant fake diamond hung from the ceiling. It must've been over twenty-five feet tall. A full orchestra played Beethoven's Fourth Symphony on the stage, above the great staircase. Clémence looked around for Livia Egle. She wasn't anywhere to be seen.

They each took a glass of champagne from the bar and admired the space. Clémence hadn't been inside the Grand Palais for years and had forgotten just how awe-inspiring it was. If the Grand Palais was a massive greenhouse, she was a humble lavender flower. Red and blue lights projected onto the glass roof. When the sky became completely dark, it was going to look incredible to the pedestrians outside.

"It's amazing, isn't it?" said Madeleine. "I haven't been here since the Chanel fashion show. There's always something crazy and interesting happening here."

"If only that was real." Clémence pointed to the huge diamond suspended in the air.

The girls admired the diamond tiaras, the glittering necklaces, and the rings, each enclosed in separate glass cases.

"Diamonds are princesses objectified," said Madeleine, who was wearing a lovely diamond necklace herself. She leaned in to whisper to Clémence, "I just hope that when Henri proposes, the ring will be as pretty as that one."

She pointed to a square pink diamond lined with smaller diamonds that belonged to a Swedish princess.

"Every girl deserves a diamond," said Clémence. "Because every girl is a princess."

Madeleine smiled at her. "You have a generous heart, you know that?"

"It's just the champagne talking," Clémence joked.

"Are you getting some ideas?" Arthur and Henri walked to the girls.

"*Oui,*" Madeleine said. "We were just window shopping."

"What have you decided on so far?" asked Henri with an amused smile.

"We both like this pink diamond," Madeleine said.

"I don't even think I'm worth as much as this diamond," said Arthur.

"Oh, you're priceless," said Clémence.

More guests filtered in during the next hour, but Livia was still nowhere to be found. Madeline and Henri were lost in the crowd, mingling, and even Arthur was enjoying a conversation with a man with salt and pepper hair. Everybody looked as if they belonged in a magazine, whether they were twenty or sixty.

Clémence did some mingling, as well, to find out if anyone knew Livia and whether she was really coming. After another half hour, she spotted Marcus Savin in the crowd, arm in arm with an equally dashing blond man. She waved to him.

"Clémence Damour!" He greeted her with bisous, then turned to his partner. "Didn't I tell you that this dress belongs on her?"

Marcus's date turned out to be his boyfriend, Brice. He greeted Clémence with bisous, as well. "This dress looks better on you than on the runway, for sure."

"I'm sorry," Marcus told her. "Livia just called me while I was getting here. I told her you wanted to talk to her, so she's open to meeting with you. The thing is, her flight got delayed, so she'll be here in forty minutes or so."

"Oh, okay. I guess that's fine." Clémence was disappointed, but she might as well enjoy the party as she waited.

"Oh look, someone's wearing my canary dress." Marcus was talking about someone behind Clémence, and she turned to look.

The woman in the silk dress had her back to them. She was speaking to a man in a tux. He was so big and imposing that he reminded Clémence of the Hulk.

"Do you know who she is?" Clémence asked.

"No."

The Hulk-like man must've told the woman they were staring at her, because she turned around.

"Come on. Let's go say hi." Marcus made his way through the crowd to her, and Brice and Clémence followed.

There was something familiar about this woman. She had long dark hair, olive skin, and big eyes, somewhat resembling the actress Penelope Cruz. Maybe that was why she looked familiar. There were a lot of people at the party that Clémence vaguely recognized.

Marcus introduced himself as the designer. "I'm so flattered to have another beautiful woman wear my dress."

"You're Marcus Savin? Wow. I was just at your store earlier. I'd buy the whole store if I could."

Marcus laughed. "You are more than welcome to."

"I'm Adana," she said. She was still smiling, with her dark eyes fixed on Clémence. "And you are?"

"Clémence Damour. *Enchantée*."

"So we're wearing the same designer!" she said. "You have good taste."

"*Merci*. So do you."

Marcus engaged Adana in a conversation about the dress for a moment. Clémence listened in, but she was distracted by the man beside Adana.

Clémence turned and looked at him. She thought there was something strange about the man, the stiff way he stood and the way his eyes avoided eye contact with any of them. With his muscles bulging out of his tight tuxedo, he looked uncomfortable and out of place at the party. His silent presence made her feel awkward, but to be polite, Clémence spoke to him.

"So, how do you know Adana?" she asked.

"Huh?"

Clémence repeated the question.

"Oh. I don't know." He spoke with a thick Spanish accent, and his French was terrible. "Excuse, I go restroom."

The man turned and walked away before Clémence could reply.

"That was odd," she muttered.

When there was lull in the conversation, Clémence asked Adana who the man was.

"I just met him actually," she said. "He says he works in the textile industry. Why?"

"Nothing. He just left abruptly."

"He's probably shy." Adana laughed. "His French is not very good. He was open with me because we were both speaking Spanish."

Clémence looked back at the man, to where he'd disappeared off to.

There was something else that had bothered her. The cologne he had been wearing smelled familiar. It had the base note of oak moss.

Chapter 13

Clémence was chatting with Adana when Marcus and Brice got pulled away by fashion designer friends they knew. Adana said she was the daughter of a Spanish film producer and had begun to do some acting herself, thanks to her connections.

"I never wanted to go into acting, but I couldn't get away from the business!" Adana laughed. "My brother works in sound design, and my sister works in costumes. I guess I had to be the actress of the family."

"You certainly look like an actress," Clémence said.

"Why, thank you. Hey, have you seen the other exhibit? It's a private showing of the more exclusive jewelry collection, not available to the public yet."

"No. Why is it private?"

"Livia was planning on taking a few select guests back there. She has a special collection of royal jewels from the Swiss Royal family."

"Is Livia a friend of yours?" Clémence asked.

"Yes, we're friends."

"Do you know when she'll be here?"

"Oh, you know Livia. She won't walk out of the door unless she's perfect. It'll be a while. Come on. I know a way into the private section."

"Will we get into trouble?"

Adana laughed and patted her arm. "You don't seem like the kind of girl who worries about getting into trouble."

Clémence wondered what that meant, but Adana seemed to have intended it as a compliment. She was curious about this private collection of jewelry, and she had time to kill. She looked around to find Madeleine, who would've surely wanted to come, but she was lost in the crowd somewhere.

Adana weaved past the display cases. Clémence followed. Adana looked around before ducking behind one display wall that featured portraits of various queens and princesses wearing their jewels.

"Clémence," she called in a high whisper. "Make sure no one is looking before you come around."

Clémence did as she was told. Once they were out of sight, Adana unhooked the velvet rope that barred them from a black door.

"Are you sure about this?" Clémence asked.

"Where's your sense of adventure?" Adana said.

When the door closed behind them, they were in pitch-black darkness.

"Adana?" Clémence didn't like this.

"Hold on." Adana rummaged through her purse.

She pulled out her smartphone, and that produced enough light to illuminate their surroundings. The walls of the room were bare.

"Where are the jewels?" Clémence asked.

As soon as she asked the question, a large hand went over her mouth. The smell of oak moss overwhelmed her. Clémence screamed, but the sweaty palm muffled all sounds. It was the man Adana had been talking to earlier, Clémence was sure of it: the Hulk.

Adana didn't seem fazed by her struggling and her attempts to scream. She let out a low chuckle.

"Where's that duct tape?" Adana muttered. She rummaged in the Hulk's pocket. He wasn't wearing his tux anymore, telling from the fabric of his sleeve.

After the sound of a rip, Adana moved his hand and slapped a piece of duct tape over Clémence's mouth.

Clémence kicked and flailed, but it didn't do any good when the man who had arms the size of tree trunks was holding her down.

"Come on. Let's hurry." Adana put on a black trench coat and put her hair up beneath a fedora hat. "Let's get this bitch in the trunk. Oh, and I'll be taking that."

She snatched away Clémence's clutch, which had her phone.

The Hulk handcuffed Clémence's hands behind her and threw her in a very large trunk. He slammed it shut.

The trunk was moved, knocking Clémence around inside. She cried. How could she have been so stupid? Why would she go off to a secluded section of the Palais with someone she barely knew just because she seemed glamorous?

Clémence should've known by now that appearances were deceiving. She just never expected the kidnapper to be a socialite around her age. What did they want with her? Who were they?

The trunk rumbled once more. She seemed to be in a moving vehicle now.

Without a watch, Clémence didn't know exactly how long she was in there for. It felt like forever.

When the trunk opened, she was looking up at a dark, starry sky.

"Get up," Adana commanded.

The Hulk pulled Clémence out and made her walk. He was dressed like a construction worker.

She was in a daze, and she felt nauseous from the car ride, but she did her best to take in her surroundings. They were in the countryside somewhere. Was it a vineyard? She couldn't tell. It was dark out, with no sign of light anywhere. As they got closer, she saw that they were walking to a small château. At least they were still in France, and they couldn't have been too far from Paris.

Vaguely knowing where she was didn't help her, however. The Hulk was too big to overtake, and she was handcuffed. She was really helpless this time. What were they going to do with her? The thought crossed her mind that they might want her because Sophie was already dead. She shuddered.

She wondered why they didn't blindfold her. Did they not care that she could see what the location looked like? A lovely French château was an odd location to store hostages. She'd assumed Sophie would be in some scary hole-in-the-wall somewhere.

When the Hulk shoved her inside the front door, she was inside an impressive foyer. Inside the trunk, she'd never expected to be taken to a locale with frescos and chandeliers and gilded mirrors.

"A summer rental," Adana remarked. "You like?"

A man ran down the stairs. "You got her! Good."

Juan.

"Yes, Diego, you got your macaron heiress," Adana said in a bored tone. She turned to the Hulk. "Take her upstairs with the other one."

The Hulk lifted Clémence up and threw her over a shoulder as if she were a sack of potatoes.

The wooden floor creaked as the Hulk thumped down a hallway and took her into a room that seemed to be the library. He sat her down in a metal chair. He unlocked one of her handcuffs and locked it to the back of the chair.

Clémence realized that Sophie was sitting in another chair, ten feet away from her. She was also handcuffed and had a piece of duct tape over her mouth. When they made contact, Clémence saw how much fear was in her eyes.

Juan kneeled by Sophie's side and began speaking in soft tones. "Everything's going to be all right. Clémence is here to replace you, so we'll be free to go now."

Sophie shook her head. Her screams were muffled by the tape.

"I know you're a little stressed at the moment," Juan continued, "but once we get away, just the two of us, we'll be back like we were."

Adana rolled her eyes. Even she thought Juan was insane. She stood over Clémence and studied her with wry amusement.

With a quick rip, the tape was torn from Clémence's mouth. She cried out in pain.

"Who are you?" Clémence demanded.

"She's my sister," said Juan.

No wonder Adana had looked familiar. Now that they were next to each other, Clémence could see the resemblance. Both of them were good looking, with sharp bone structure, dark eyes lined with thick lashes, and plush lips. The thought crossed her mind that they were too good looking to be doing the cruel things they were doing.

"*Half*-sister," Adana insisted. "We're just a bunch of nobodies."

"What do you want?" Clémence asked.

"It's simple what I want," she said. "Money. We were doing a decent job of kidnapping spoiled heiresses until Diego here had to go and fall in love with one of them. Oh puke."

"I just couldn't do that to Sophie's family." Juan's eyes were those of a madman. "We're fated. Star-crossed lovers, like Romeo and Juliet."

"Oh, you're pathetic," Adana snapped. "She'll never love you, after what you've done to her. Why can't you get that through your dumb head?"

Juan stood up. "You're wrong. She'll understand in time. She really does love me."

"Then why don't we remove the duct tape from her mouth again and see what the little bitch says?"

Juan sputtered. "She doesn't know what she's saying right now. She's just shocked. Like I said, once we're away together, she'll remember how in love we are. Now that you've got your heiress for your ransom, I'm taking Sophie."

Adana let out a loud cackle. "Not so fast."

"What?" Juan demanded. "You said that once you got the heiress, you'll let me have my girl."

"Come on, Juan, don't you see we have an even better opportunity here? We'll get twice as much money from two rich families. This will be our last kidnapping, and we'll never have to do this again."

Juan looked from Clémence to Sophie. Once again, he kneeled down next to Sophie. "No, I need Sophie. She's my life now!"

Adana shrugged and laughed again. "Suit yourself." She nodded to the Hulk, who remained stone faced.

Slowly, the Hulk reached into his back pocket and pulled out a gun.

Chapter 14

Juan's eyes widened. He backed away, looking furiously between Adana and the Hulk.

"Wait—what are you guys doing?"

"You've been a nuisance long enough, Diego," Adana said in her cold, calm voice. "This was supposed to be simple. You seduce one of these rich bimbos, we get the money, and we move on. Now that you've become a weak link, we have to get rid of you."

"But—but I'm your brother."

"Oh please. I never liked your mother. She spoiled you rotten. And that bitch never liked me. What did you expect? You really think we'd be dumb enough to let the girl go free? You just had to take off her blindfold. She knows what we look like. She knows where she is. You're stupid if you don't think that the first place she's going to run to when she's freed is the police station!"

"No. She won't. Sophie loves me!"

"Look how insane you are!" Adana said, even though she was laughing like a madwoman herself.

"You're crazy and delusional. The girl is terrified. And she should be. Like I said, this is our last job. Once we get the money from these girls, we don't have to do this ever again. Bobby and I will have enough money to retire for the rest of our lives."

"Adana," Juan croaked. "Please—"

"Do it, Bobby."

The Hulk obliged and shot Juan in the chest. He stumbled around for a couple of seconds before falling at the girls' feet. Sophie's screams once again were muffled by the tape. Clémence only looked away.

The Hulk put the gun away and started pulling Juan's feet to drag him away.

"Oh, leave him," Adana commanded. "Let the girls enjoy the view for a bit. Ugh, I need to get out of this ugly dress." She glared at Clémence. "Yes, I followed you into the store earlier. I thought sharing the same designer would be a good icebreaker, but you found me first. Stupid girl. We were going to take you yesterday, but you were lucky your boyfriend was hanging around your bed. Maybe we would've taken him, too, if there were more people—competent people—on my team. Instead, we found your phone in the living room and I bugged it so we could hear what you were up to. Not bad for a girl who never finished high school, don't you think? How does it feel to be checkmated by a girl who couldn't even read until the fifth grade?"

Clémence stayed silent, knowing whatever she said wouldn't matter. She had to stay silent so she wouldn't be beaten or killed.

After Adana's laughter subsided, she jerked around to face the Hulk. "Hey, I'm starved. There was barely any good food at that dumb party. Let's go eat. Got any leftovers, or do we have to eat at that crappy Italian restaurant nearby again?"

She stormed out, and the Hulk followed, locking the door behind him with a key. Her heels clunked down the stairs, followed by the Hulk's heavy thuds.

Sophie was crying. Her eyes were closed and her head turned away from the dead body by their feet.

Clémence had seen enough bodies to get used to them—somewhat. She looked around desperately for an escape, a solution, anything.

As soon as the kidnappers got the money from their parents, they were going to kill both of them.

They were both handcuffed to chairs. Nobody knew where they were. Nobody could hear their screams. Her phone was taken away from her—her phone...

She wondered if Juan's phone was still on his person.

She looked down and noticed a bulge in Juan's pant pocket. Could that be it?

Taking a deep breath, she kicked off her heels. With a big toe, she nudged whatever it was out of the pocket.

Sure enough, it was his smartphone. Clémence wanted to squeal from excitement. She prayed. This was their only chance.

With both feet, she turned the phone so that the screen was facing up.

Her breathing turned heavy. She was anxious and too afraid to hope. With a big toe she pressed on the Home button on the phone.

The phone was unlocked.

Chapter 15

They didn't have to wait long before the police showed up. They ambushed Adana and the Hulk by surprise in the kitchen while they were eating the dessert portion of their dinner—homemade crêpes. The Hulk was multi-talented; he also knew how to cook.

While they were being arrested, Sophie and Clémence were uncuffed. When her hands were freed, Sophie peeled off the tape from her mouth, but she didn't say anything. She just sobbed and put her face in her hands.

The police gave them a ride back into the city.

"Are you okay?" Clémence asked Sophie in the car.

Sophie gave an exasperated sigh. Her breath smelled funky, and she hadn't showered for days. The tears still hadn't dried on her cheeks. "I don't even know where to begin to explain how I'm feeling," she said in a small voice.

"I understand," said Clémence. "You don't have to say anything right now."

Having fallen for Juan/Carlos/Diego once, Clémence could easily have been in Sophie's place. Even though Diego professed genuine love to Sophie in the end, how much would that mean coming from a con artist, a kidnapper, and a madman? To add more fuel to the fire, he was killed by his sister, who was crazy in her own right.

In the Paris police station, Arthur rushed to Clémence as soon as they came in. He held her in a tight embrace.

"You crazy, crazy girl," he whispered. "I thought I lost you."

Clémence felt numb after what she'd been through, but she knew that Sophie had it much, much worse. Sophie couldn't stop crying into Madeleine's shoulder. Theo was there too, and he stood beside the girls in silent support.

"I'm sorry I didn't keep an eye on you at the party," Arthur continued. "I just let you out of my sight. I thought you were safe in the crowd."

"It's my own fault," Clémence said. "My own curiosity gets me into a lot of dangerous messes. I should be sorry for worrying you. I guess we're never safe anywhere, huh? But at least it all worked out in the end."

"You're the most dangerous part of my life, you nut. I'd hate you if I didn't love you."

Clémence looked up at him. "You love me?"

Arthur smiled and nodded. Clémence hugged him tighter.

Sophie's parents came around and they thanked her, and so did Madeleine. Sophie only looked at her with tear-brimmed eyes, and that was all the thanks Clémence needed.

Then the familiar lanky figure of Inspector Cyril St. Clair loomed over her.

"Well, you did it. You almost got yourself killed."

"I did," Clémence calmly agreed.

"But you've also inadvertently solved the case."

He shook her hand. That was the extent of his kindness.

Clémence couldn't help but smile. "It's my job to make your job easier. I should be getting paid for this."

"You're lucky you're not thrown in jail for all the ruckus you've caused in recent months," he quipped.

He asked her a series of questions about the evening's events. After speaking for over an hour, she had trouble keeping her eyelids open.

"I'm exhausted," Clémence said, "and I've told you everything you need to know. Can we go now?"

"Yes, fine." Cyril turned to Arthur. "Be careful with this girl. She can't seem to stay out of trouble."

"You don't need to tell me," Arthur replied.

Clémence took out her smartphone, which had been given back to her by the police, and called a taxi.

After saying good-bye to the Seydoux family, Clémence stood up to go. Madeleine hugged her and told her she'd get in touch soon.

With Arthur's arm around her shoulders, she walked out the front entrance. To their surprise, a crowd of paparazzi and news cameras were waiting outside.

"*Merde*," Arthur swore under his breath. "Why didn't they warn us they were here?"

News must've finally spread about the kidnapping. Clémence looked down and realized she was still in Marcus Savin's lavender dress. It was torn in places and a little dirty. She probably wouldn't be able to return it now. At least she held up her end of the bargain by being photographed in the dress. But she wasn't going to be recognized in the papers the next day for wearing a Marcus Savin dress. Clémence would be known as the heiress who was kidnapped.

Recipe #1

Thin Crêpes & Filling Ideas

Sweet crêpes are like French-style pancakes. They can be eaten for breakfast, dessert, or as snacks. The French enjoy crêpes so much that they sometimes throw crêpe parties. A variety of ingredients are available to guests so they can make the crêpe of their choice.

Thin Crêpe Recipe

makes about 13–15 crêpes

- 1 cup all-purpose flour
- 2 eggs
- 1 1/2 cups milk
- 2 tbsp sugar
- 1/2 tsp vanilla extract

- 1 tbsp unsalted butter, melted
- Butter for cooking

Combine flour, sugar and salt in a bowl. Add eggs, vanilla and half of the milk. Stir with a whisk until smooth. Add remaining half of milk, stirring constantly. Whisk in melted butter.

Preheat a non-stick skillet or a frying pan. When the skillet is hot, brush with butter.

Use 3 tablespoons of batter for each crêpe. Pour it in the center and tilt the skillet to spread the batter evenly. When the edge begins to brown and peel off easily, flip the crêpe with a spatula. Continue cooking for 10 seconds and then remove from skillet.

Stack them on a plate as you cook them. Cover with aluminum foil to keep them warm and from drying. If you have leftovers, you can store them in the fridge after wrapping them in plastic, and reheat them when you are ready to eat them again.

You can use a variety of fillings. Here are some ideas to use alone or to combine as you desire:

- jam
- Nutella
- whipped cream
- chocolate sauce

- ice cream

- sliced bananas

- raspberries

- strawberries

- blueberries

- dark chocolate

- nuts

- nut butter

- maple syrup

My personal favorite combination is Nutella with sliced bananas and whipped cream.

Recipe # 2

Whole Wheat Crêpes

Here is a healthier, whole-wheat alternative.

Makes 13–15 crêpes

- 1 cup whole wheat pastry flour
- 1/2 cup buttermilk
- 1/2 cup water
- 2 egg whites
- 2 tsp olive oil
- 1/4 tsp salt
- Non-stick cooking spray

Blend smooth the first six ingredients in a blender or food processor. Refrigerate for 1 hour or up to 8 hours covered.

Heat a skillet over medium heat. Coat with cooking spray. Transfer 3 to 4 tablespoons of batter onto the skillet. Spread with a small spoon or spatula. Cook for 2 to 3 minutes until the edges are brown and it starts to dry out on top. Flip and cook the other side for another 2 minutes.

Recipe #3

Gluten Free Crêpes

A gluten-free alternative for those with gluten allergies. The recipe is for only 5 because they are meant for immediate consumption. If they're left out for more than 20 minutes, they start to become chewy.

Makes 5 crêpes

- 1 cup brown rice flour
- egg substitute for 3 eggs
- 1/2 cup water
- 1 tablespoon vegetable oil

Mix all ingredients in a bowl. Use just enough water so that the batter is smooth.

Pour a small amount in a skillet or frying pan. Tilt skillet so the batter speeds across the pan. Flip and cook the other side.

They should be slightly golden brown when done.

Recipe #4

Crêpes Suzette

This is an old-school French classic and the most famous crêpe flavor. Crêpe Suzette is a sweet crêpe flambéed with orange liqueur. They can be ordered from five-star restaurants, but here's a simple enough recipe for you to master at home.

- 2 tbsp unsalted butter
- 3 tbsp granulated sugar
- 1/3 cup orange juice
- 3 tbsp orange liqueur (Grand Marnier)
- 2 tbsp grated orange rind
- 4 crêpes (see Recipe #1 to #3)

Melt sugar with butter in a skillet over medium heat. Add orange rind, orange juice and 1 tbsp of orange liqueur and bring to a boil. Reduce heat and simmer for 1 minute.

Add 1 crêpe to the skillet. Turn to coat. Use tongs to fold crêpe into quarters. Move crêpe to side of skillet. Repeat with remaining crêpes, overlapping around the edge of the pan. Drizzle with remaining liqueur. Remove from heat and ignite pan. When flames subside, serve crêpes.

Recipe #5

Chocolate Crêpes

makes 10

- 10 crêpes (Choose from recipes #1 to #3)

Filling:

- 1 package of cream cheese (8 ounces), softened
- 1/4 cup sugar
- 1/2 cup sour cream
- 1/2 tsp vanilla extract
- 1/3 crème de cacao
- 1 carton (8 ounces) frozen whipped cream, thawed

Fudge Sauce:

- 3/4 cup semi-sweet chocolate chips

- 1/3 cup butter
- 1/2 cup sugar
- 2/3 cup half-and-half cream

For filling: Beat cream cheese and sugar until light and fluffy. Beat in sour cream and vanilla. Fold in crème of cacao and whipped cream. Cover and refrigerate for at least 1 hour.

For fudge sauce: Melt chocolate chips and butter over low heat. Stir in sugar and cream. Bring to a boil. Reduce heat, uncovered, for 10 minutes.

Spoon 1/4 cup filling down the center of each crêpe and then roll up. Drizzle fudge sauce over each crêpe.

Recipe #6

Savory Buckwheat Crêpes & 4 Fillings

Savory crêpes, also known as galettes, make great breakfasts and lunches. The thin crêpe allows the filling to fill you up.

While all the crêpe recipes listed here so far can be used for savory crêpes, buckwheat crêpes are commonly used because they naturally lend to savory flavors. This recipe makes 4 crêpes.

- 2/3 cup buckwheat flour
- 1/3 cup all-purpose flour
- 3 large eggs
- 5 tbsp unsalted butter + butter for cooking
- 1 3/4 cups whole milk

- 1/2 tsp salt

Melt 5 tablespoons of butter in a non-stick skillet. Combine the melted butter (then set skillet aside), both flours, milk, eggs, and salt in a blender until smooth. Let batter rest at room temperature for at least 1 hour or overnight.

Preheat the oven to 300 degrees F. Heat the skillet over medium heat until hot. Butter skillet lightly. Add 1/3 cup of batter, quickly swirling to coat the bottom of the pan. Cook for about 2 minutes, until the crêpe sets and the edges brown. Flip over and cook for about 30 more seconds. Transfer to a plate.

Repeat with the remaining batter, adding more butter as needed. Stack finished crêpes on a plate. They can be covered in plastic and refrigerated, then reheated before eating.

You can serve buckwheat crêpes with a variety of fillings. Here are some French ideas:

Crêpes Montagnardes: cooked potato slices, ham, sliced Reblochon cheese.

Quatre Fromages: a 4-cheese mix of Emmental, Comté, Camembert, and blue cheese. After filling the crêpe, bake crêpe for a few minutes to melt the cheese.

Crêpes Océanes: sliced salmon topped with crème fraîche and fresh dill.

Chèvre et Lardons: Goat cheese and chopped cooked bacon.

The possibilities are endless with sweet and savory crêpes. Now that you know how to make the crêpes, the fillings are only limited to your imagination.

Bon appétit!

About the Author

Harper Lin lives in Kingston, Ontario with her family. When she's not reading or writing mysteries, she's in yoga class, hiking, or hanging out with her family and friends. *The Patisserie Mysteries* draws from Harper's own experiences of living in Paris in her twenties. She is currently working on more cozy mysteries.

www.HarperLin.com

Harper Lin

Crêpe Murder

Made in the USA
Middletown, DE
29 July 2016